The Forsaken Inn by Anna Katharine Green

Anna Katharine Green was born in Brooklyn, New York on November 11th, 1846.

Anna's initial ambition was to be a poet. However that path failed to ignite any significant interest and she turned to fiction writing. She published her first—and most famous work in 1878—'The Leavenworth Case'. Wilkie Collins praised it and it sold extremely well.

It led to Anna writing 40 novels and to becoming known as 'the mother of the detective novel.'

In helping to shape the genre she brought many other innovations including a series detective: her main character was detective Ebenezer Gryce of the New York Metropolitan Police Force, but in three novels he is assisted by the nosy society spinster Amelia Butterworth, another innovation and a prototype for Miss Marple, Miss Silver and others.

She also invented the 'girl detective': in the character of Violet Strange, a debutante with a secret life as a sleuth. Anna's other innovations included the now familiar dead bodies in libraries, newspaper clippings as "clews," the coroner's inquest, and expert witnesses. Yale Law School once used her books to demonstrate how damaging it can be to rely on circumstantial evidence.

Her career was now well advanced and she was much admired.

On November 25, 1884, Green married the actor and stove designer, and later noted furniture maker, Charles Rohlfs, who was seven years her junior. They had three children; Rosamund, Roland and Sterling.

Although Anna was a progressive she did not approve of many of her feminist contemporaries, and was opposed to women's suffrage.

On November 25, 1884, Anna married the actor and noted furniture maker, Charles Rohlfs, who was seven years her junior. They had three children; Rosamund, Roland and Sterling.

Anna Katharine Green died on April 11, 1935 in Buffalo, New York, at the age of 88.

Index of Contents

CHAPTER I

THE OAK PARLOR

I was riding between Albany and Poughkeepsie. It was raining furiously, and my horse, already weary with long travel, gave unmistakable signs of discouragement. I was, therefore, greatly relieved when, in the most desolate part of the road, I espied rising before me the dim outlines of a house, and was correspondingly disappointed when, upon riding forward, I perceived that it was but a deserted ruin I was approaching, whose fallen chimneys and broken windows betrayed a dilapidation so great that I could scarcely hope to find so much as a temporary shelter therein.

Nevertheless, I was so tired of the biting storm that I involuntarily stopped before the decayed and forbidding structure, and was, in truth, withdrawing my foot from the stirrup, when I heard an unexpected exclamation behind me, and turning, saw a chaise, from the open front of which leaned a gentleman of most attractive appearance.

"What are you going to do?" he asked.

"Hide my head from the storm," was my hurried rejoinder. "I am tired, and so is my horse, and the town, according to all appearances, must be at least two miles distant."

"No matter if it is three miles! You must not take shelter in that charnel-house," he muttered; and moved along in his seat as if to show me there was room beside him.

"Why," I exclaimed, struck with sudden curiosity, "is this one of the haunted houses we hear of? If so, I shall certainly enter, and be much obliged to the storm for driving me into so interesting a spot." I thought he looked embarrassed. At all events, I am sure he hesitated for a moment whether or not to ride on and leave me to my fate. But his better impulses seemed to prevail, for he suddenly cried: "Get in with me, and leave mysteries alone. If you want to come back here after you have learned the history of that house, you can do so; but first ride on to town and have a good meal. Your horse will follow easily enough after he is rid of your weight."

It was too tempting an offer to be refused; so thankfully accepting his kindness, I alighted from my horse, and after tying him to the back of the chaise, got in with this genial stranger. As I did so I caught another view of the ruin I had been so near entering.

"Good gracious!" I exclaimed, pointing to the structure that, with its projecting upper story and ghastly apertures, presented a most suggestive appearance, "if it does not look like a skull!"

My companion shrugged his shoulders, but did not reply. The comparison was evidently not a new one to him.

That evening, in a comfortable inn parlor, I read the following manuscript. It was placed in my hands by this kindly stranger, who in so doing explained that it had been written by the last occupant of the old inn I was so nearly on the point of investigating. She had been its former landlady, and had clung to the ancient house long after decay had settled upon its doorstep and desolation breathed from its gaping windows. She died in its north room, and from under her pillow the discolored leaves were taken, the words of which I now place before you.

JANUARY 28, 1775.

I do not understand myself. I do not understand my doubts nor can I analyze my fears. When I saw the carriage drive off, followed by the wagon with its inexplicable big box, I thought I should certainly regain my former serenity. But I am more uneasy than ever. I cannot rest, and keep going over and over in my mind the few words that passed between us in their short stay under my roof. It is her face that haunts me. It must be that, for it had a strange look of trouble in it as well as sickness; but neither can I forget his, so fair, so merry, and yet so unpleasant, especially when he glanced at her and—as I could not help but think before they went away—when he glanced at me. I do not like him, and the chills creep over me whenever I remember his laugh, which was much too frequent to be decent, considering how poorly his young wife looked.

They are gone, and their belongings with them; but I am as much afraid as if they were still here. Why? That is what I cannot tell. I sit in the room where they slept, and feel as strange and terrified as if I had encountered a ghost there. I dread to stay and dread to move and write, because I must relieve myself in some way—that is, if I am to have any sleep to-night. Am I ill, or was there something unexplained and mysterious in their actions? Let me go over the past and see.

They came last evening about twilight. I was in the front of the house, and seeing such a good-looking couple in the carriage, and such a pile of baggage with them that they had to have an extra wagon to carry it, I ran out in all haste to welcome them. She had a veil drawn over her face, and it was so thick that I could not see her features, but her figure was slight and graceful, and I took a fancy to her at once, perhaps because she held her arms out when she saw me, as if she thought she beheld in me a friend. He did not please me so well, though there is no gainsaying that he is handsome enough, and speaks, when he wishes to, with a great deal of courtesy. But I thought he ought to give his attention to his young and ailing wife, instead of being so concerned about his baggage. Had that big box of his contained gold, he could not have looked at it more lovingly or been more anxious about its handling. He said it held books; but, pshaw! what is there in books, that a man should love them better than his wife, and watch over their welfare with the utmost concern, while allowing a stranger to help her out of the carriage and up the inn steps?

But I will not dwell any longer upon this. Men are strange beings, and must not be judged by rules that apply to women. Let me see if I can remember when it was that I first saw her face. Ah, yes; it was in the parlor. She had taken a seat there while her husband looked through the house and decided which room to take. There were four empty, and two of them were the choicest and airiest in the inn, but he passed by these and insisted upon taking one that was stuffy with disuse, because it was on the ground floor, and so convenient for us to bring his great box into.

His great box! I was so provoked at this everlasting concern about his great box, that I ran to the parlor, intending to ask the lady herself to interfere. But when I got to the threshold I paused, and did not speak, for the lady—or Mrs. Urquhart, as I presently found she called herself—had risen from her seat and was looking in the glass with an expression so sad and searching that I forgot my errand and only thought of comforting her. But the moment she heard my step she drew down the veil which she had tossed back, and coming quickly toward me, asked if her husband had chosen a room.

I answered in the affirmative, and began to complain that it was not a very cheerful one. But she paid small attention to my words, and presently I found myself following her to the apartment designated. She entered, making a picture, as she crossed the threshold, which I shall not readily forget. For in her short, quick walk down the hall she had torn the bonnet from her head, and though she was not a strictly beautiful woman, she was sufficiently interesting to make her every movement attractive. But that is not all. For some reason the moment possessed an importance for her which I could not measure. I saw it in her posture, in the pallor of her cheeks and the uprightness of her carriage. The sudden halt she made at the threshold, the half-startled exclamation she gave as her eyes fell on the interior, all showed that she was laboring under some secret agitation. But what was the cause of that agitation I have not been able to determine. She went in, but as she did so, I heard her murmur:

"Oak walls! Ah, my soul! it has come soon!"

Not a very intelligible exclamation, you will allow, but as intelligible as her whole conduct. For in another moment every sign of emotion had left her, and she stood quite calm and cold in the center of the room. But her pallor remained, and I cannot make sure now whether this betokened weary resignation or some secret and but half recognized fear.

Had I looked at him instead of at her, I might have understood the situation better. But, though I dimly perceived his form drawn up in the empty space at the left of the door, it was not until she had passed him and flung herself into a chair, that I thought to look in his direction. Then it was too late, for he had turned his face aside and was gazing with rather an obtrusive curiosity at the old-fashioned room, murmuring, as he did so, some such commonplaces to his wife as:

"I hope you are not fatigued, my dear. Fine old house, this. Quite English in style, eh?"

To all of which she answered with a nod or word, till suddenly, without look or warning, she slipped from her chair and lay perfectly insensible upon the dark boards of the worm-eaten floor.

I uttered an exclamation, and so did he; but it was my arms that lifted her and laid her on the bed. He stood as if frozen to his place for a moment, then he mechanically lifted his foot and set it with an air of proprietorship on the box before which he had been standing.

"Strange and inexplicable conduct," thought I, and looked the indignation I could not but feel. Instantly he left his position and hastened to my side, offering his assistance and advice with that heartless officiousness which is so unbearable when life and death are at stake.

I accepted as little of his help as was possible, and when, after persistent effort on my part, I saw her lids fluttering and her breast heaving, I turned to him with as inoffensive an air as my mingled dislike and distrust would admit, and asked how long they had been married. He flushed violently, and with a sudden rage that at once robbed him of that gentlemanly appearance which, in him, was but the veneer to a coarse and brutal nature, he exclaimed:

"—you! and by what right do you ask that?"

But before I could reply he recovered himself and was all false polish again, bowing with exaggerated politeness, as he exclaimed:

"Excuse me; I have had much to disturb me lately. My wife's health has been very feeble for months, and I am worn out with anxiety and watching. We are now on our way to a warmer climate, where I hope she will be quite restored."

And he smiled a very strange and peculiar smile, that went out like a suddenly extinguished candle, as he perceived her eyes suddenly open, and her gaze pass reluctantly around the room, as if forced to a curiosity against which she secretly rebelled.

"I think Mrs. Urquhart will do very well now," was his hurried remark at this sight. He evidently wished to be rid of me, and though I hated to leave her, I really found nothing to say in contradiction to his statement, for she certainly looked completely restored. I therefore turned away with a heavy heart toward the door, when the young wife, suddenly throwing out her arms, exclaimed:

"Do not leave me in this horrible room alone! I am afraid of it—actually afraid! Couldn't you have found some spot in the house less gloomy, Edwin?"

I came back.

"There are plenty of rooms—" I began.

But he interrupted me without any ceremony.

"I chose this room, Honora, for its convenience. There is nothing horrible about it, and when the lamps are lit you will find it quite pleasant. Do not be foolish. We sleep here or nowhere, for I cannot consent to go upstairs."

She answered nothing, but I saw her eyes go traveling once again around the walls, followed in a furtive way by his. Whereupon I looked about me, too, and tried to get a stranger's impression of the place. I was astonished at its effect upon my imagination. Though I had been in and out of the room fifty times before I had never noticed till now the extreme dismalness and desolation of its appearance.

Once used as an auxiliary parlor, it had that air of uninhabitableness which clings to such rooms, together with a certain something else, equally unpleasant, to which at that moment I could give no name, and for which I could neither find then nor now any sufficient reason. It was paneled with oak far above our heads, and as the walls above had become gray with smoke, there was absolutely no color in the room, not even in the hangings of the gaunt four-poster that loomed dreary and repelling from one end of the room. For here, as elsewhere, time had been at work, and tints that were once bright enough had gradually been subdued by dust and smoke into one uniform dimness. The floor was black, the fireplace empty, the walls without a picture, and yet it was neither from this grayness nor from this barrenness that one recoiled. It was from something else—something that went deeper than the lack of charm or color—something that clung to the walls like a contagion and caught at the heart-strings where they are weakest, smothering hope and awakening horror, till in each faded chair a ghost seemed sitting, gazing at you with immovable eyes that could tell tales, but would not.

There was but one window in the room, and that looked toward the west. But the light that should have entered there was frightened, also, and halted on the ledge without, balked by the thick curtains that heavily enshrouded it. A haunted chamber! or so it appeared at that moment to my somewhat excited fancy, and for the first time in my life, here, I felt a dread of my own house, and experienced the uncanny sensation of some one walking over my grave.

But I soon recovered myself. Nothing of a disagreeable nature had ever happened in this room, nor had we had any special reason for shutting it up, except that it was in an out-of-the-way place, and not usually considered convenient, notwithstanding Mr. Urquhart's opinion to the contrary.

"Never mind," said I, with a last effort to soothe the agitated woman. "We will let in a little light, and dissipate some of these shadows." And I attempted to throw back the curtains of the window, but they fell again immediately and I experienced a sensation as of something ghostly passing between us and the light.

Provoked at my own weakness, I tore the curtains down and flung them into a corner. A straggling beam of sunset color came in, but it looked out of place and forlorn upon that black floor, like a stranger who meets with no welcome. The poor young wife seemed to hail it, however, for she moved instantly to where it lay and stood as if she longed for its warmth and comfort. I immediately glanced at the fireplace.

"I will soon have a rousing fire for you," I declared. "These old fireplaces hold a large pile of wood."

I thought, but I must be mistaken, that he made a gesture as if about to protest, but, if so, reason must have soon come to his aid, for he said nothing, though he looked uneasy, as I moved the andirons forward and made some other trivial arrangements for the fire which I had promised them.

"He thinks I am never going," I muttered to myself, and took pleasure in lingering; for, anxious as I was to have the room heated up for her comfort, I knew that every moment I stayed there would be one less for her to spend with her surly husband alone.

At last I had no further excuse for remaining, and so with the final remark that if the fire failed to give them cheer we had a sitting room into which they could come, I went out. But I knew, even while saying it, that he would not grant her the opportunity of enjoying the sitting room's coziness; that he would not let her out of his sight, if he did out of the room, and that for her to remain in his presence was to be in darkness, solitude and gloom, no matter what walls surrounded her or in what light she stood.

My impressions were not far wrong. Mr. and Mrs. Urquhart came to supper, but that was all. Before the others had finished their roast they had eaten their pudding and gone; and though he had talked, and laughed, and shown his white teeth, the impression left behind them was a depressing one which even Hetty felt, and she has anything but a sensitive nature.

I went to the room once again in the evening. I found them both seated, but in opposite parts of the room; he by his great box, and she in an easy chair which I had caused to be brought down from my own room for her especial use. I did not look at him, but I did at her, and was astonished to see, first, how dignified she was; and next how pretty. Had she been happy and at her ease, I should probably have been afraid of her, for the firelight, which now shone on her wan young cheek, brought out evidences of character and culture in her expression which proved her to be, by birth and training, of a position superior to what one would be led to expect from her husband's aspect and manner. But she was not happy nor at her ease, and wore, instead of the quiet and commanding look of the great lady, such an expression of secret dread that I almost forgot my position of landlady, and should certainly, if he had not been there, fallen at her side and taken her poor, forsaken head upon my breast. But that silent, immovable form, sitting statue-like beside his big box, smiling, for aught I knew, but if so, breathing out a chill that forbade all exhibition of natural feeling, held me in check, as it held her, so that I merely inquired whether there was anything I could do for her; and when she shook her head, starting a tear down her cheek as she did so, I dared do nothing more than give her one look of sympathetic understanding, and start for the door.

A command from him stopped me.

"My wife will need a slight supper before she goes to bed," said he. "Will you be good enough to see that one is brought?"

She roused herself up with quite a startled look of wonder.

"Why, Edwin," she began, "I never have been in the habit—"

But he hushed her at once.

"I know what is best for you," said he. "A small plate of luncheon, Mrs. Truax; and let it be nice and inviting."

I courtesied, gave her another glance, and went out. Her countenance had not lost its look of wonder. Was he going to be considerate, after all?

The lunch was prepared and taken to her.

Not long after this the inn quieted down, and such guests as were in the house prepared for rest. Midnight came; all was dark in room and hall. I was sure of this, for I went through the whole building myself, contrary to my usual habit, which was to leave this task to my man-of-all-work, Burritt. All was dark, all was quiet, and I was just dropping off to sleep, when there shot up suddenly from below a shriek, which was quickly smothered, but not so quickly that I did not recognize in it that tone which is only given by hideous distress or mortal fear.

"It is Mrs. Urquhart!" I cried in terror, to myself; and plunging into my clothes, I hurried down stairs.

CHAPTER II

BURRITT

All was quiet in the halls, but as I proceeded toward their room I perceived a figure standing near the doorway, which, in another moment, I saw to be that of Burritt. He was trembling like a leaf, and was bent forward, listening.

"Hush!" he whispered; "they are talking. All seems to be right. I just heard him call her darling."

I drew the man away and took his place. Yes; they were talking in subdued but not unkindly tones. I heard him bid her be composed, and caught, as I thought, a light reply that ought to have satisfied me that Mrs. Urquhart had simply suffered from some nightmare horror at which she was as ready to laugh now as he. But my nature is a contradictory one, and I was not satisfied. The echo of her cry was still ringing in my ears, and I felt as if I would give the world for a momentary peep into their room. Influenced by this idea, I boldly knocked, and in an instant—too soon for him not to have been standing near the door—I heard his breath through the keyhole and the words:

"Who is there, and what do you want?"

"We heard a cry," was my response, "and I feared Mrs. Urquhart was ill again."

"Mrs. Urquhart is very well," came hastily, almost gayly, from within. "She had a dream, and was willing that every one should know it. Is not that all?" he said, seemingly addressing his wife.

There was a murmur within, and then I heard her voice. "It was only a dream, dear Mrs. Truax," it said, and convinced against my will, I was about to return to my room, when I brushed against Burritt. He had not moved, and did not look as if he intended to.

"Come," said I, "there is no use of our remaining here."

"Can't help it," was his whispered reply. "In this hall I stay till morning. When I see a lamb in the care of a wolf, I find it hard to sleep. There is a door between us, but please God there shan't be anything more."

And knowing Burritt, I did not try to argue, but went quietly and somewhat thoughtfully to my room, vaguely relieved that I left him behind, though convinced there would be no further need of his services.

And so it was. No more sounds disturbed the house, and when I came down, with the first streak of daylight, I found Burritt gone about his work.

Breakfast was served to the Urquharts in their own room. I had wished to carry it in myself, but I found this inconvenient, and so I sent Hetty. When she came back I asked her how Mrs. Urquhart looked.

"Very well, ma'am," was the quick reply. "And see! I don't think she's as unhappy as we all thought last night, or she wouldn't be giving me a bright new crown."

I glanced at the girl's palm. There was indeed a bright new crown in it.

"Did she give you that?" I inquired.

"Yes, ma'am; she herself. And she laughed when she did it, and said it was for the good breakfast I had brought her."

I was busy at the time, and could not stop to give the girl's words much thought; but as soon as I had any leisure, I went to see for myself how Mrs. Urquhart looked when she laughed.

I was five minutes too late. She had just donned her traveling bonnet and veil, and though I heard her laugh slightly once, I did not see her face.

I saw his, however, and was surprised at the good nature in it. He was quite the gentleman, and if he had not been in such a hurry, would have doubtless made, or endeavored to make, himself very agreeable. But he was just watching his great box carried out to the wagon, and while he took pains to talk to me—was it to keep me from talking to her?—he was naturally a little absentminded. He was in haste, too, and insisted upon placing his wife in the carriage before all his baggage was taken from the room. And she seemed willing to go. I watched her on purpose to see, for I was not yet satisfied that she was not playing a part at his dictation, but I could discover no hint of reluctance in her manner, but rather a quiet alacrity, as if she felt glad to quit a room to which she had taken a dislike.

When I saw this, and noted the light step of her feet, I said to myself that I had been a fool, and lost a little of the interest I had felt for her. Nor did I regain it till after they had driven away, though she showed a consideration for me at the last which I had not expected, leaning from the carriage to give me a good-by pressure of the hand, and even nodding again and again as they disappeared down the road. For the fear which could be dissipated in a night was not the fear with which I had credited her; and of ordinary excitements and commonplace natures I had seen enough in my long experience as landlady to make me unwilling to trouble myself with any more of them.

But when the carriage and its accompanying wagon had quite disappeared, and Mr. and Mrs. Urquhart were virtually as far beyond my reach as if they were already in New York, I became conscious of a great uneasiness. This was the more strange in that there seemed to be no especial cause for it. They had left my house in apparently better spirits than they had entered it, and there was no longer any reason why I should concern myself about them. And yet I did concern myself, and came into the house and into the room they had just vacated, with feelings so unusual that I was astonished at myself, and not a little provoked. I had a vague feeling that the woman who had just left was somehow different from the one I had seen the night before.

But I am a busy woman, and I do not think I should have let this trouble me long if it had not been for Burritt. But when he came into the room after me, and shut the door behind him and stood with his back against it, looking at me, I knew I was not the only one who felt uncomfortable about the Urquharts. Rising from the chair where I had been sitting, counting the cost of fitting up that room so as to make it look habitable, I went toward him and met his gaze pretty sharply.

"Well, what is it?" I asked.

"I don't know," was the somewhat sullen reply. "I don't feel right about those folks, and yet—" He stopped and scratched his head—"I don't know what I'm afraid of. Are you sure they left nothing behind them?"

The last words were uttered in such a tone I did not know for a minute what to say.

"Left anything behind them!" I replied. "They left their money, if that is what you mean. I don't know what else they could have left."

Notwithstanding which assertion, I involuntarily glanced about the room as if half expecting to see some one of their many belongings protruding from a hitherto unsearched corner. His gaze followed mine, but presently returned, and we stood again looking at each other.

"Nothing here," said I.

"Where is it, then?" he asked.

I frowned in displeasure.

"Where is what?" I demanded. "You speak like a fool. Explain yourself."

He took a step toward me and lowered his voice. Every one knows Burritt, so I need not describe him. You can all imagine how he looked when he said:

"Did you see me handling of the big box, ma'am?"

I nodded yes.

"Saw how I was the one to help carry it in, and also how I was the one to first take hold on it when he wanted it carried out?" I again nodded yes.

"Well, ma'am, that box was a heavy load to lift into the wagon, but, ma'am"—here his voice became quite sepulchral—"it wasn't as heavy as it was when we lifted it out, and it hadn't the same feel either. Now, what had happened to it, and where is the stuff he took out of it?"

I own I had never in my life felt creepy before that minute. But with his eyes staring at me so impressively, and his voice sunk to a depth that made me lean forward to hear what he had to say, I do declare I felt as if an icy breath had been blown across the roots of my hair.

"Burritt, you want to frighten me," I exclaimed, as soon as I could get my voice. "The box seemed heavier to you than it did just now. There was no change in it, there could not be, or we should find something here to account for it. Remember you did not sleep last night, and lack of rest makes one fanciful."

"It does not make a man feel stronger, though, and I tell you the box was not near so heavy to-day as yesterday. Besides, as I said before, it acted differently under the handling. There was something loose in it to-day. Yesterday it was packed tight."

I shook my head, and tried to throw off the oppression caused by his manner. But seeing his eyes travel to the window, I looked that way too.

"He didn't carry anything out of the door," declared Burritt, at this moment, "because I watched it, and I know. But that window is only three feet from the ground, and I remember now that at the instant I first laid my ear to the keyhole, I heard a strange, grating sound just like that of a window being lowered by a very careful hand. Shall I look outside it, ma'am?"

I replied by going quickly to the window myself, lifting it, which I did with very little trouble, and glancing out. The familiar garden, with its path to the river, lay before me; but though I allowed myself one quick look in its direction, it was to the ground immediately beneath the window that I turned my attention, and it was here that I instantly, and to the satisfaction of both Burritt and myself, discovered unmistakable signs of disturbance. Not only was there the impression of a finely booted foot imprinted in the loose earth, but there was a large stone lying against the house which we were both confident had not been there the day before.

"He went roaming through the garden last night," cried Burritt, "and he brought back that stone. Why?"

I shuddered instead of replying. Then remembering that I had seen the young wife well and happy only a few minutes before, felt confused and mystified beyond any power to express.

"I will have a look at that stone," continued Burritt; and without waiting for my sanction, he vaulted out of the window and lifted the stone.

After a moment's consideration of it he declared:

"It came from the river bank; that is all I can make out of it."

And dropping the stone from his hand, he suddenly darted down the path to the river.

He was not gone long. When he came back, he looked still more doubtful than before.

"If I know that bank," he declared, "there has been more than one stone taken from it, and some dirt. Suppose we examine the floor, ma'am."

We did so, and just where the box had been placed we discovered some particles of sand that were not brought in from the road.

"What does it mean?" I cried.

Burritt did not answer. He was looking out toward the river. Suddenly he turned his eyes upon me and said in his former suppressed tone:

"He filled the box with stone and earth, and these were what we carried out and put into the wagon. But it was full when it came, and very heavy. Now, what was it filled with, and what has become of the stuff?"

It was the question then; it is the question now.

Burritt hints at crime, and has gone so far as to spend all the afternoon searching the river banks. But he has discovered nothing, nor can he explain what it was he looked for or expected to find. Nor are my own thoughts and feelings any clearer. I remember that the times are unsettled, that the spirit of revolution is in the air, and try to be charitable enough to suppose that it was treasure the young husband brought with him, and that all the perturbation and distress which I imagine myself to have witnessed in his behavior and that of his wife were owing to the purpose that they had formed of burying, in this spot, the silver and plate which they were perhaps unwilling to risk to the chances of war. But when I try to stifle my graver fears with this surmise, I recall the fearful nature of the shriek which startled me from my sleep, and repeat, tremblingly, to myself:

"Some one was in mortal agony at the moment I heard that cry. Was it the young wife, or was it—"

CHAPTER III

A FEARFUL DISCOVERY

APRIL 3, 1791.

It is sixteen years since I wrote the preceding chapters of this history of mystery and crime. When the pen dropped from my hand—why did it drop? Was it because of some noise I heard?

I imagine so now, and tremble. I did not anticipate ever adding a line to the words I had written. The impulse which had led me to put upon paper my doubts concerning the two Urquharts soon passed, and as nothing ever occurred to recall this couple to my mind, I gradually allowed their name and memory to vanish from my thoughts, only remembering them when chance led me into the oak parlor. Then, indeed, I recollected their manner and my fears, and then I also felt repeated, though every time with fainter and fainter power, the old thrill of undefined terror which stopped my record of that day with the half-finished question as to who had uttered the shriek that had startled me the night before. To-day I again take up my pen. Why? Because to-day, and only since to-day, can I answer this question.

Sixteen years ago! which makes me sixteen years older. My house, too, has aged, and the oak parlor—I never refurnished it—is darker, gloomier, and more forbidding than it was then, and in truth, why should it not be? When I remember what was revealed to me a week ago, I wonder that its walls did not drop fungi, and its chill strike death through the man or woman who was brave enough to enter it. Horrible, horrible room! You shall be torn from my house if the rest of the structure goes with you. Neither I nor another shall ever enter your fatal portal again.

It was a week ago to-day that the coach from New York set down at my door a stranger of fine and quaint appearance, whose white hair betokened him to be aged, but whose alert and energetic movements showed that, if he had passed the line of fourscore, he had still enough of the fire of youth remaining to make his presence welcome in whatever place he chose to enter. As had happened sixteen years before, I was looking out of the window when the coach drove up, and, being at once attracted by the stranger's person and manner, I watched him closely while he was alighting, and was surprised to observe what intent and searching glances he cast at the house.

"He could not be more interested if he were returning to the home of his fathers," I murmured involuntarily to myself, and hastened to the door in order to receive him.

He came forward courteously. But after the first few words between us he turned again and gazed with marked curiosity up and down the road and again at the house.

"You seem to be acquainted with these parts," I ventured. He smiled.

"This is an old house," he answered, "and you are young." (I am fifty-five.) "There must have been owners of the place before you. Do you know their names?"

"I bought the place of Dan Forsyth, and he of one Hammond. I don't know as I can go back any further than that. Originally the house was the property of an Englishman. There were strange stories about him, but it was so long ago that they are almost forgotten."

The stranger smiled again, and followed me into the house. Here his interest seemed to redouble.

Instantly a thought flashed through my brain.

"He is its ancient owner, the Englishman. I am standing in the presence of—"

"You wish to know my name," interrupted his genial voice. "It is Tamworth. I am a Virginian, and hope to stay at your inn one night. What kind of a room have you to offer me?"

There was a twinkle in his eyes I did not understand. He was looking down the hall, and I thought his gaze rested on the corridor leading to the oak parlor.

"I should like to sleep on the ground floor," he added.

"I have but one room," I began.

"And one is all I want," he smiled. Then, with a quick glance at my face: "I suppose you are a little particular whom you put into the oak parlor. It is not every one who can appreciate such romantic surroundings."

I surveyed him, completely puzzled. Whereupon he looked at me with an expression of surprise and incredulity that added to the mystery of the moment.

"The room is gloomy and uninviting," I declared; "but beyond that, I do not know of any especial claim it has upon our interest."

"You astonish me," was his evidently sincere reply; and he walked on, very thoughtfully, straight to the room of which we were speaking. At the door he paused. "Don't you know the secret of this room," he asked, giving me a very bright and searching glance.

"If you mean anything concerning the Urquharts," I began doubtfully.

"Urquharts!" he carelessly repeated. "I do not know anything about them. I am speaking of an old tradition. I was told—let me see how long it is now—well, it must be sixteen years at least—that this house contained a hidden chamber communicating with a certain oak parlor in the west wing. I thought it was curious, and—Why, madam, I beg your pardon; I did not mean to distress you. Can it be possible that you were ignorant of this fact?—you, the owner of this house!"

"Are you sure it is a fact?" I gasped. I was trembling in every limb, but managed to close the door behind us before I sank into a chair. "I have lived in this house twenty years. I know its rooms and halls as I do my own face, and never, never have I suspected that there was a nook or corner in it which was not open to the light of day. Yet—yet it is true that the rooms on this floor are smaller than those above, this one especially." And I cast a horrified glance about me, that reminded me, even against my will, of the searching and peculiar look I had seen cast in the same direction by Mr. Urquhart sixteen years before.

"I see that I have stumbled upon a bit of knowledge that has been kept from the purchasers of this property," observed the old gentleman. "Well, that does not detract from the interest of the occasion. When I knew I was to pass this way, I said to myself I shall certainly stop at the old inn with the secret chamber in it, but I did not think I should be the first one to disclose its secret to the present generation. But my information seems to affect you strangely. Is it such a disturbing thing to find that one's house has held a disused spot within it, that might have been made useful if you had known of its existence?"

I could not answer. I was enveloped in a strange horror, and was only conscious of the one wish—that Burritt had lived to help me through the dreadful hour I saw before me.

"Let us see if my information has been correct," continued Mr. Tamworth. "Perhaps there has been some mistake. The secret chamber, if there is one, should be behind this chimney. Shall I hunt for an opening?"

I managed to shake my head. I had not strength for the experiment yet. I wanted to prepare myself.

"Tell me first how you heard about this room?" I entreated.

He drew his chair nearer to mine with the greatest courtesy.

"There is no reason why I should not tell you," replied he, "and as I see that you are in no mood for a long story, I shall make my words as few as possible. Some years ago I had occasion to spend a night in an inn not unlike this, on Long Island. I was alone, but there was a merry crowd in the tap room, and being fond of good company, I presently found myself joining in the conversation. The talk was of inns, and many a stirring story of adventure in out-of-the-way taverns did I listen to that night before the clock struck twelve. Each man present had some humorous or thrilling experience to relate, with the exception of a certain glum and dark-browed gentleman, who sat somewhat apart from the rest, and who said nothing. His reticence was in such marked contrast to the volubility about him that he finally attracted universal attention, and more than one of the merry-makers near him asked if he had not some anecdote to add to the rest. But though he replied with sufficient politeness, it was evident that he had no intention of dropping his reserve, and it was not till the party had broken up and the room was nearly cleared that he deigned to address any one. Then he turned to me, and with a very peculiar smile, remarked:

"'A dull collection of tales, sir. Bah! if they had wanted to hear of an inn that was really romantic, I could have told them—'

"'What?' I involuntarily ejaculated. 'You will not torture me by suggesting a mystery you will not explain.'

"He looked very indifferent.

"'It is nothing,' he declared, 'only I know of an inn—at least it is used for an inn now—which has in its interior a secret chamber so deftly hidden away in the very heart of the house that I doubt if even its present owner could find it without the minutest directions from the man who saw it built. I knew that man. He was an Englishman, and he had a fancy to make his fortune through the aid of smuggled goods. He did it; and though always suspected, was never convicted, owing to the fact that he kept all his goods in this hidden room. The place is sold now, but the room remains. I wonder if any forgotten treasures lie in it. Imagination could easily run riot over the supposition, do you not think so, sir?'

"I certainly did, especially as I imagined myself to detect in every line of his able and crafty face that he bore a closer relation to the Englishman than he would have me believe. I did not betray my feelings, however, but urged him to tell me how in a modern house, a room, or even a closet, could be so concealed as not to awaken any one's suspicion. He answered by taking out pencil and paper, and showing me, by a few lines, the secret of its construction. Then seeing me deeply interested, he went on to say:

"'We find what we have been told to search for; but here is a case where the secret has been so well kept that in all possibility the question of this room's existence has never arisen. It is just as well.'

"Meantime I was studying the plan.

"'The hidden chamber lies,' said I, 'between this room,' designating one with my forefinger, 'and these two others. From which is it entered?'

"He pointed at the one I had first indicated.

"'From this,' he affirmed. 'And a quaint, old-fashioned room it is, too, with a wainscoting of oak all around it as high as a man's head. It used to be called the oak parlor, and many a time has its floor rung to the tread of the king's soldiers, who, disappointed in their search for hidden goods, consented to take a drink at their host's expense, little recking that, but a few feet away, behind the carven chimneypiece upon which they doubtless set down their glasses, there lay heaps and heaps of the richest goods, only awaiting their own departure to be scattered through the length and breadth of the land.'

"'And this house is now an inn?' I remarked.

"'Yes.'

"'Curious. I should like nothing better than to visit that inn.'

"'You doubtless have.'

"'It is not this one?' I suddenly cried, looking uneasily about me.

"'Oh, no; it is on the Hudson River, not fifty miles this side of Albany. It is called the Happy-Go-Lucky, and is in a woman's hands at present; but it prospers, I believe. Perhaps because she has discovered the secret, and knows where to keep her stores.' And with a shrug of his shoulders he dismissed the subject, with the remark: 'I don't know why I told you of this. I never made it the subject of conversation before in my life.'

"This was just before the outbreak in Lexington, sixteen years ago, ma'am, and this is the first time I have found myself in this region since that day. But I have never forgotten this story of a secret room, and when I took the coach this morning I made up my mind that I would spend the night here, and, if possible, see the famous oak parlor, with its mysterious adjunct; never dreaming that in all these years of your occupancy you would have remained as ignorant of its existence as he hinted and you have now declared."

Mr. Tamworth paused, looking so benevolent that I summoned up my courage, and quietly informed him that he had not told me what kind of a looking man this stranger was.

"Was he young?" I asked. "Had he a blond complexion?"

"On the contrary," interrupted Mr. Tamworth, "he was very dark, and, in years, as old or nearly as old as myself."

I was disappointed. I had expected a different reply. As he talked of the stranger, I had, rightfully or wrongfully, with reason or without reason, seen before me the face of Mr. Urquhart, and this description of a dark and well-nigh aged man completely disconcerted me.

"Are you certain this man was not in disguise?" I asked.

"Disguise?"

"Are you certain that he was not young, and blond, and—"

"Quite sure," was the dry interruption. "No disguise could transform a young blood into the man I saw that night. May I ask—"

In my turn I interrupted him. "Pardon me," I entreated, "but an anxiety I will presently explain forces another question from me. Were you and this stranger alone in the room when you held this conversation? You say that it had been full a few minutes before. Were there none of the crowd remaining besides your two selves?"

Mr. Tamworth looked thoughtful. "It is sixteen years ago," he replied, "but I have a dim remembrance of a man sitting at a table somewhat near us, with his face thrown forward on his arms. He seemed to be asleep; I did not notice him particularly."

"Did you not see his face?"

"No."

"Was he young?"

"I should say so."

"And blond?"

"That I cannot say."

"And he remained in that attitude all the time you were talking?"

"Yes, madam."

"And continued so when you left the room?"

"I think so."

"Was he within earshot? Near enough to hear all you said?"

"Most assuredly, if he listened."

"Mr. Tamworth," I now entreated, "try, if possible, to remember one other fact. If each man present told a story that night, you must have had ample opportunity of noting each man's face and observing how he looked. Now, of all that sat in the room, was there not one of an age not exceeding thirty-five, of fair complexion and gentlemanly appearance, yet with a dangerous look in his small blue eye, and a something in his smile that took all the merriment out of it?"

"A short but telling description," commented my guest. "Let me see. Was there such a man among them? Really, I cannot remember."

"Think, think. Hair very thin above the temples, mustache heavy. When he spoke he invariably moved his hands; seemed to be nervous, and anxious to hide it."

"I see him," was Mr. Tamworth's sudden remark. "That description of his hands recalls him to my mind. Yes; there was such a man in the room that night. I even recollect his story. It was coarse, but not without wit."

I advanced and surveyed Mr. Tamworth very earnestly. "The man you thought asleep—the man who was near enough to hear all the Englishman said—was he or was he not the same we have just been talking about?"

"I never thought of it before, but he did look something like him—his figure, I mean; I did not see his face."

"It was he," I murmured, with intense conviction, "and the villain—" But how did I know he was a villain? I paused and pointed to the huge mantel guarding the fireplace. "If you know how to enter the secret room, do so. Only I should like to have a few witnesses present besides myself. Will you wait till I call one or two of my lodgers?"

He bowed with great urbanity. "If you wish to make the discovery public," said he, "I, of course, have no objection."

But I saw that he was disappointed.

"I can never confront the secret of that room alone," I insisted. "I must have Dr. Kenyon here at least." And without waiting for my impulses to cool, I sent a message to the doctor's room, and was rewarded in a moment by the appearance at the door of that excellent man.

It did not take many words for me to explain to him our intentions. We were going to search for a secret chamber which we had been told opened into the room in which we then found ourselves. As I did not wish to make any mystery of the affair, and as I naturally had my doubts as to what the room might disclose, I asked the support of his presence.

He was gratified—the doctor always is gratified at any token of appreciation—and perceiving that I had no further reason for delay, I motioned to Mr. Tamworth to proceed.

How he discovered the one movable panel in that old-fashioned wainscoting, I have never inquired. When I saw him turn toward the fireplace and lay his ear to the wall, I withdrew in haste to the window, feeling as if I could not bear to watch him, or be the first to catch a glimpse of the mysterious depths which in another moment must open before his touch. What I feared I cannot say. As far as I could reason on the subject, I had no cause to fear anything; and yet my shaking frame and unevenly throbbing heart were but the too sure tokens of an excessive and uncontrollable agitation. The view from the window increased it. Before me lay the river from whose banks sand and stone had been taken sixteen years before to replace—what? I knew no more this minute than I did then. I might know in the next. By the faint tapping that came to my ears I must—and it was this thought that sent a chill through me, and made it so difficult for me to stand. And yet why should it? Was not that old theory of ours, that the Urquharts had brought treasure in their great box, still a plausible one? Nay, more, was it not even a probable one, since we had discovered that the house held so excellent a hiding place, unknown to the world at large, but known to this man, as Mr. Tamworth's story so plainly showed? Yes; and yet I started with uncontrollable forebodings, when I heard an exclamation of satisfaction behind me, and hardly found courage to turn around, even when I knew that an opening had been effected, and that they were only waiting for my approach to enter it.

And it took courage, both on my part and on theirs; for the air which rushed from the high and narrow slit of darkness before us was stifling and almost deadly. But in a few minutes, after one or two experiments with a lighted candle, Dr. Kenyon stepped through the opening, followed by Mr. Tamworth, and, in a long minute afterward, by myself.

Shall I ever forget my emotions as I looked about me and saw, by the lamp which the doctor carried, nothing more startling than an old oak chest in one corner, a pile of faded clothing in another, and in a third—Heavens! what is it? We all stare, and then a shriek escapes my lips as piercing and terror-stricken as any that ever disturbed those fearful shadows; and I rush blindly from the spot, followed by Mr. Tamworth, whose face, as I turn to look at him, gives me another pang of fear, so white and sick it looks in the sudden glare of day.

Worse than I had thought, worse than I had dreamed! I cannot speak, and fall into a chair, waiting in mortal terror for the doctor, who stayed some minutes behind. When his kindly but not undisturbed countenance showed itself again in the gap at the side of the fireplace, I could almost have thrown myself at his feet.

"What is it?" I gasped. "Tell me at once. Is it a man or a woman or—"

"It is a woman. See! here is a lock of her hair. Beautiful, is it not? She must have been young."

I stared at it like one demented. It was of a peculiar reddish-brown, with a strange little kink and curl in it. Where had I seen such hair before? Somewhere. I remembered perfectly how the whole bright head looked with the firelight playing over it. Oh, no, no, no, it was not that of Mrs. Urquhart. Mrs. Urquhart went away from this house well and happy. I am mad, or this strand of gleaming hair is a dream. It is not her head it recalls to me, and yet—my soul, it is!

The doctor, knowing me well, did not try to break the silence of that first grewsome minute. But when he saw me ready to speak, he remarked:

"It is an old crime, perpetrated, probably, before you came into the house. I would not make any more of it than you can help, Mrs. Truax."

I scarcely heeded him.

"Is there no bit of clothing or jewelry left upon her by which we might hope to identify her?" I asked, shuddering, as I caught Mr. Tamworth's eye, and realized the nature of the doubts I there beheld.

"Here is a ring I found upon the wedding finger," he replied. "It was doubtless too small to be drawn off at the time of her death, but it came away easily enough now."

And he held out a plain gold circlet which I eagerly took, looked at, and fell at their feet as senseless as a stone.

On the inner surface I had discovered this legend:

E. U. to H. D. Jan. 27, 1775.

CHAPTER IV

QUESTIONS AND ANSWERS

Never have I felt such relief as when, upon my resuscitation, I remembered that I had put upon paper all the events and all the suspicions which had troubled me during that fatal night of January the 28th, sixteen years before. With that in my possession, I could confront any suspicion which might arise, and it was this thought which lent to my bearing at this unhappy time a dignity and self-possession which evidently surprised the two gentlemen.

"You seem more shocked than astonished," was Mr. Tamworth's first remark, as, mistress once more of myself, I led the way out of that horrible room into one breathing less of death and the charnel house.

"You are right," said I. "Mysteries which have troubled me for years are now in the way of being explained by this discovery. I knew that something either fearful or precious had been left in the keeping of this house or grounds; but I did not know what this something was, and least of all did I suspect that its hiding place was between walls whose turns and limitations I thought I knew as well as I do the paths of my garden."

"You speak riddles," Dr. Kenyon now declared. "You knew that something fearful or precious had been left in your house—"

"Pardon me," I interrupted; "I said house or grounds. I thought it was in the grounds, for how could I think that the house could, without my knowledge, hold anything of the nature I have just suggested?"

"You knew, then, that a person had been murdered?"

"No," I persisted, with a strange calmness, considering how agitated I was, both by my memories and the fears I could not but entertain for the future; "I know nothing; nor can I, even with the knowledge of this discovery, understand or explain what took place in my house sixteen years ago."

And in a few hurried words I related the story of the mysterious couple who had occupied that room on the night of January 27, 1775.

They listened to me as if I were repeating a fairy tale, and as I noted the sympathizing air with which Dr. Kenyon tried to hide his natural incredulity, I again congratulated myself that I had been a weak enough woman to keep an account of the events which had so impressed me.

"You think I am drawing upon my imagination," I quietly remarked, as silence fell upon my narration.

"By no means," the doctor began, hurriedly; "but the details you give are so open to question, and the conclusions you expect us to draw from them are so serious, that I wish, for your own sake, we had heard something of the Urquharts, and your doubts and suspicions in their regard, before we had made the discovery which points to death and crime. You see I speak plainly, Mrs. Truax."

"You cannot speak too plainly, Doctor Kenyon; and my opinion so entirely coincides with yours that I am going to furnish you with what you ask." And without heeding their looks of astonishment, I rang the bell for one of the girls, and sent her to a certain drawer in my desk for the folded paper which she would find there.

"Here!" I exclaimed, as the paper was brought, "read this, and you will soon see how I felt about the Urquharts on the evening of the day they left us."

And I put into their hands the record I had made of that day's experience.

While they were reading it, I puzzled myself with questions. If this body which we had just found sepulchered in my house was, as the initials in the ring seemed to declare, that of Honora Urquhart, who was the woman who passed for her at the time of the departure of this accused couple from my doors? I was with them, and saw the lady, and supposed her to be the same I had entertained at my table the night before. But then I chiefly noted her dress and height, and did not see her face, which was hidden by her veil, and did not hear her voice beyond the short and somewhat embarrassed laugh she gave at some little incident which had occurred. But Hetty had seen her, and had even received money from her hand; and Hetty could not have been deceived, nor was Hetty a girl to be bribed. How was I, then, to understand the matter? And where, in case another woman had taken Mrs. Urquhart's place, had that woman come from?

I thought of the low window, and the ease with which any one could climb into it; and then, with a flash of startled conviction, I thought of the huge box.

"Great heavens!" I ejaculated, feeling the hair stir anew on my forehead. "Can it be that he brought her in that? That she was with them all the time, and that the almost hellish tragedy to which this ring points was the scheme of two vile and murderous lovers to suppress an unhappy wife that stood in the way of their desires?"

I could not think it. I could not believe that any man could be so void of mercy, or any woman so lost to every instinct of decency, as to plan, and then coolly carry out to the end, a crime so unheard of in its atrocity. There must be some other explanation of the facts before us. Why, the date in the ring is enough. If that speaks true, the marriage between Edwin Urquhart and the gentle Honora was but a day old, and even the worst of men take time to weary of their wives before they take measures against them. Yet, the look and manner of the man! His affection for the box, and his manifest indifference for his wife! And, lastly, and most convincing of all, this awful token in the room beyond! What should I, what could I think!

At this point in my surmises I grew so faint that I turned to Dr. Kenyon and Mr. Tamworth for relief. They had just finished my record of the past, and were looking at each other in surprise and horror.

"It surpasses the most atrocious deeds of the middle ages," quoth Mr. Tamworth.

"In a country deemed civilized," finished the doctor.

"Then you think," I tremblingly began—

"That you have harbored two demons under your roof, Mrs. Truax. There seems to be no doubt that the woman who went away with Mr. Urquhart was not the woman who came with him. She lies here, while the other—"

He paused, and Mr. Tamworth took up the word.

"It seems to have been a strangely triumphant piece of villainy. The woman who profited by it must have had great self-control and force of character. Don't you think so, doctor?"

"Unquestionably," was the firm reply.

"You do not say how you account for her presence here," I now reluctantly intimated.

"I think she was hidden in the great box. It was large enough for that, was it not, Mrs. Truax?"

I nodded, much agitated.

"His care of it, his call for a supper, the change in its weight, and the fact that its contents were of a different character in going than coming, all point to the fact of its having been used for the purpose we intimated. It strikes one as most horrible, but history furnishes us with precedents of attempts equally daring, and if the box was well furnished with holes—did you notice any breathing places in it?"

"No," I returned; "but I did not cast two glances at the box. I was jealous of it, for the young wife's sake, though, as God knows, I had little idea of what it contained, and merely noticed that it was big and clumsy, and capable of holding many books."

"Yet you must have noticed, even in a cursory glance, whether its top or sides were broken by holes."

"They were not, but—"

"But what?"

"I do remember, now, that he flung his traveling-cloak across it just as the men went to lift it from the wagon, and that the cloak remained upon it all the time it was in their hands, and until after we had all left the room. But it was taken away later, for when I went in the second time, I saw it lying across the chair."

"And the box?"

"Was hidden by the foot of the bed behind which he had dragged it."

"And the cloak? Was it over the box when it went out?"

"No; but I have thought since we have been talking, that the box might have been turned over after its occupant left it. The holes, if there were any, would thus be on the bottom, and would escape our detection."

"Very possible, but the sand with which we supposed the box had been filled would have sifted through."

"Not if a good firm piece of stuff was laid in first, and there were plenty of such in the secret chamber."

"That is true. But Burritt, you write, was listening at the door, and yet you mention no remarks of his concerning any noises heard by him from within. And noise must have been made if this was done, as it must have had to be done after the tragedy."

"I know I do not," was the hurried reply. "But Burritt probably did not remain at the door all the time. There is a window seat at the end of the corridor, and upon it he probably lolled during the few hours of his watch. Besides, you must remember that Burritt left his post some time before daylight. He had his duties to attend to, some of which necessitated his being in the stables by four o'clock, at least."

"I see; and so the affair prospered, as most very daring deeds do, and they escaped without suspicion, or rather without suspicion pointed enough to lead to their being followed. I wonder where they escaped to, and if in all the years that have elapsed, they have for one moment imagined that they were happy."

"Happy!" was my horrified exclamation. "Oh, if I could find them! If I could drag them both to this room and make them keep company with their victim for a week, I should feel it too slight a retribution for them."

"Heaven has had its eye upon them. We have been through fearful crises since that day, and much unrighteous as well as righteous blood has been shed in this land. They may both be dead."

"I do not believe it," I muttered. "Such wretches never die." Then, with a renewed remembrance of Hetty, I remarked: "Curses on the duties that kept me out of this room on that fatal morning. Had I seen the woman's face, this horrid crime would at least been spared its triumph. But I was obliged to send Hetty, and she saw nothing strange in the woman, though she received money from her hand, and—"

"Where is Hetty?" interrupted the doctor.

"She is married, and lives in the next town."

"So, so. Well, we must hunt her up to-morrow, and see what she has to say about the matter now."

But we soon found ourselves too impatient to wait till the morrow, so after we had eaten a good supper in a cheerful room, Dr. Kenyon mounted his horse, and rode away to the farm house where Hetty lived. While he was gone, Mr. Tamworth summoned up courage to re-enter that cave of horror, and bring out the contents of the oak chest we had seen there. These were mostly stuffs in a more or less good state of preservation, and all the assistance they lent to the understanding of the tragedy that mystified us was the fact that the chest contained nothing, nor the room itself, of sufficient substance to help the wicked Urquhart in giving weight to the box which he had emptied of its living freight. This is doubtless the reason he resorted to the garden for the sand and stone he found there.

Dr. Kenyon returned about midnight, and was met at the door by Mr. Tamworth and myself.

"Well?" I cried, in great excitement.

"Just as I supposed," he returned. "She did not see the lady's face either. The latter was in bed, and the girl took it for granted that the arm and hand which reached her out a silver piece from between the bed curtains were those of Mrs. Urquhart."

"My house is cursed!" was my sudden exclamation. "It has not only lent itself to the success of the most demoniacal scheme that ever entered into the heart of man, but it has kept its secret so long that all hope of explaining its details or reaching the guilty must be abandoned."

"Not so," quoth Mr. Tamworth. "Though an old man, I dedicate myself to this task. You will hear again of the Urquharts."

CHAPTER V

AN INTERIM OF SUSPENSE

MAY 5, 1791.

How fearful! To hear a spade in the night and know that this spade is digging a grave! I sit at my desk and listen to hear if any one in the house has been aroused or is suspicious, and then I turn to the window and try to pierce the gloom to see if anything can be discerned, from the house, of the grewsome act now being performed in the garden. For after much consultation and several conferences with the authorities, we have decided to preserve from public knowledge, not only the secret of the room hidden in my house, but of the discovery which has lately been made there. But while much harm would accrue to me by revelations which would throw a pall of horror over my inn, and make it no better than a place of morbid curiosity forever, the purposes of justice would be rather hindered than helped by a publicity which would give warning to the guilty couple, and prevent us from surprising them in the imagined security which the lapse of so many years must have brought them.

And so a grave is being dug in the garden, where, at the darkest hour of night, the remains of the sweet and gentle bride are to be placed without tablet or mound.

Meanwhile do there hide in any part of this wicked world two hearts which throb with unusual terrors this night? Or does there pass across the mirror of a guilty memory any unusual shapes of horror prognostic of detection and coming punishment? It would comfort my uneasy heart to know; for the spirit of vengeance has seized upon me, and my house will never seem washed of its stain, or my conscience be quite at rest as to the past, till that vile man and woman pay, in some way, the penalty of their crime.

That we know nothing of them but their names lends an interest to their pursuit. The very difficulty before us, the hopelessness almost of the task we have set ourselves, have raised in me a wild and well-nigh superstitious reliance on Providence and the eternal justice, so that it seems natural for me to expect aid even from such sources as dreams and visions, and make the inquiry in which I have just indulged the reasonable expression of my belief in the mysterious forces of right and wrong, which will yet bring this long triumphant, but now secretly threatened, pair to justice.

Dr. Kenyon, who is as practical as he is pious, smiles at my confidence; but Mr. Tamworth neither mocks nor frowns. He has shouldered the responsibility of finding this man, and has often observed, in his long life, that a woman's intuitions go as far as a man's reasoning.

To-morrow he will start upon his travels.

JUNE 12, 1791.

It is foolish to put every passing thought on paper, but these sheets have already served me so well that I cannot resist the temptation of making them the repositories of my secret fears and hopes. Mr. Tamworth has been gone a month, and I have heard nothing from him. This is all the more difficult to bear that Dr. Kenyon also has left me, thus taking from my house all in whom I can confide or to whom I can talk. For I will not place confidence in servants, and there are no guests here at present upon whose judgment I can rely concerning even a lesser matter than this which occupies all my thoughts.

I must talk, then, to thee, unknown reader of these lines, and declare on paper what I have said a thousand times to myself—what a mystery this whole matter is, and how little probability there is of our ever understanding it! Why was it that Edwin Urquhart, if he loved one woman so well that he was willing to risk his life to gain her, would subject himself to the terrors which must follow any crime, no matter how secretly performed, by marrying a woman he must kill in twenty-four hours? Marriages are not compulsory in this country, and any one must acknowledge that it would be easier for a strong man—and he certainly was no weakling—to refuse a woman at the nuptial altar than to undertake and carry out a scheme so full of revolting details and involving so much risk as this which we have been forced to ascribe to him.

Then the woman, the unknown and fearful creature who had allowed herself to be boxed up and carried, God knows, how many fearful miles, just for the purpose of assuming a position which she seemingly might have obtained in ways much less repulsive and dangerous! Was it in human nature to go through such an ordeal, and if it were, what could the circumstances have been that would drive even the most insensible nature into such an adventure! I question, and try to answer my own inquiries, but my imagination falters over the task, and I am no nearer to the satisfaction of my doubts than I was in the harrowing minute when the knowledge of this tragedy first flashed upon me.

I must have patience. Mr. Tamworth must write to me soon.

AUGUST 10, 1791.

News, news, and such news! How could I ever have dreamed of it! But let me transcribe Mr. Tamworth's letter:

To Mrs. Clarissa Truax, Mistress of the Happy-go-lucky Inn:

RESPECTED MADAM: After a lengthy delay, occupied in researches, made doubly difficult by the changes which have been wrought in the country by the late conflict, I have just come upon a fact that has the strongest bearing upon the serious tragedy which we are both so interested in investigating. It is this:

That every year the agent of a certain large estate in Albany, N. Y., forwards to France a large sum of money, for the use and behoof of one Honora Quentin Urquhart, daughter of the late Cyrus Dudleigh, of Albany, and wife of one Edwin Urquhart, a gentleman of that same city, to whom she was married in her father's house on January 27, 1775, and with whom she at once departed for France, where she and her husband have been living ever since.

Thus by chance, almost, have I stumbled upon an explanation of the tragedy we found so inexplicable, and found that clew to the whereabouts of the wretched pair which is so essential to their apprehension and the proper satisfaction of the claims of justice.

With great consideration I sign myself,

Your obedient servant, ANTHONY TAMWORTH.

AUGUST 11, 8 o'clock.

I was so overwhelmed by the above letter that I found it impossible at the time to comment upon it. To-day it is too late, for this morning a packet arrived from Mr. Tamworth containing another letter of such length that I am sure it must be one of complete explanation. I burn to read it, but I have merely had time to break the seal and glance at the first opening words. Will my guests be so kind as to leave me in peace to-night, so that I may satisfy a curiosity which has become almost insupportable?

MIDNIGHT.

No time to-night; too tired almost to write this.

AUGUST 12.

The packet is read. I am all of a tremble. What a tale! What a— But why encumber these sheets with words of mine? I will insert the letter and let it tell its own portion of the strange and terrible history which time is slowly unrolling before us.

PART II

AN OLD ALBANY ROMANCE

CHAPTER VI

THE RECLUSE

To Mrs. Clarissa Truax, of the Happy-go-lucky Inn:

RESPECTED MADAM: Appreciating your anxiety, I hasten to give you the particulars of an interview which I have just had with a person who knew Edwin Urquhart. They must be acceptable to you, and I shall make no excuse for the length of my communication, knowing that each detail in the lives of the three persons connected with this crime must be of interest to one who has brooded upon the subject as long as you have.

The person to whom I allude is a certain Mark Felt, a most eccentric and unhappy being now living the life of a recluse amid the forests of the Catskills. I became acquainted with his name at the time of my first investigation into the history of the Dudleigh and Urquhart families, and it was to him I was referred when I asked for such particulars as mere neighbors and public officials found it impossible to give.

I was told, however, at the same time, that I should find it hard to gain his confidence, as for sixteen years now he had avoided the companionship of men, by hiding in the caves and living upon such food as he could procure through the means of gun and net. A disappointment in love was said to be at the bottom of this, the lady he was engaged to having thrown herself into the river at about the time of the marriage of his friend.

He was, notwithstanding, a good-hearted man, and if I could once break through the reserve he had maintained for so many years, they thought I would be able to surprise facts from him which I could never hope to reach in any other way.

Interested by these insinuations, and somewhat excited, for an old man, at the prospect of bearding such a lion in his den, I at once made up my mind to seek this Felt; and accordingly one bright day last week crossed the river and entered the forest. I was not alone. I had taken a guide who knew the location of the cave which Felt was supposed to inhabit, and through his efforts my journey was made as little fatiguing as possible. Fallen brambles were removed from my path, limbs lifted, and where the road was too rough for the passage of such faltering feet as mine, I found myself lifted bodily, in arms as strong and steadfast as steel, and carried like a child to where it was smoother.

Thus I was enabled to traverse paths that at first view appeared inaccessible, and finally reached a spot so far up the mountain side that I gazed behind me in terror lest I should never be able to return again the way I had come. My guide, seeing my alarm, assured me that our destination was not far off, and presently I perceived before me a huge overhanging cliff, from the upper ledges of which hung down a tangle of vines and branches that veiled, without wholly concealing, the yawning mouth of a cave.

"That is where the man we are seeking lives, eats, and sleeps," quoth my guide, as we paused for a moment to regain our breath. And immediately upon his words, and as if called forth by them, we perceived an unkempt and disheveled head slowly uprear itself through the black gap before us, then hastily disappear again behind the vines it had for a moment disturbed.

"I will encounter him alone," I thereupon declared; and leaving the guide behind me, I pushed forward to the cliff, and pausing before the entrance of the cave, I called aloud:

"Mark Felt, do you want to hear news from your friend Urquhart?"

For a moment all was still, and I began to fear that my somewhat daring attempt had failed in its effect. But this was only for an instant, for presently something between a growl and a cry issued from the darkness within, and the next moment the wild and disheveled head showed itself again, and I heard distinctly these words:

"He is no friend of mine, your Edwin Urquhart."

"Then," I returned, without a moment's hesitation, "do you want to hear news of your enemy?—for I have some, and of the rarest nature, too."

The wild eyes flashed as if a flame of fire had shot from them, and the head that held them advanced till I could see the whole bearded countenance of the man.

"Is he dead?" he asked, with an eagerness and underlying triumph in the voice that argued well for the presence of those passions upon the rousing of which I relied for the revelations I sought.

"No," said I, "but death is looking his way. With a little more knowledge of his early life and a little more insight into his character at the time he married Honora Dudleigh, the law will have so firm a hold upon him that I can safely promise any one who longs to see him pay the penalty of his evil deeds a certain opportunity of doing so."

The vines trembled and suddenly parted their full length, and Mark Felt stepped out into the sunshine and confronted me. What he wore I cannot say, for his personality was so strong I received no impression of anything else. Not that he was tall or picturesque, or even rudely handsome. On the contrary, he was as plain a man as I had ever seen, with eyes to which some defect lent a strange, fixed glare, and a mouth whose under jaw protruded so markedly beyond the upper that his profile gave you a shock when any slight noise or stir drew his head to one side and thus revealed it to you. Yet, in spite of all this, in spite of tangled locks and a wide, rough beard, half brown, half white, his face held something that fixed the attention and fascinated the eye that encountered it. Did it lie in his eyes? How could it, with one looking like a fixed stone of agate and the other like a rolling ball of fire? Was it in his smile? How could it be when his smile had no joy in it, only a satisfaction that was not of good, but evil, and promised trouble rather than relief or sympathy? It must be in the general expression of his features, which seemed made only to mirror the emotions of a soul full of vitality and purpose—a soul which, if clouded by wrongs and embittered by heavy memories, possessed at least the characteristic of force and the charm of an unswerving purpose.

He seemed to recognize the impression he had made, for his lips smiled with a sort of scornful triumph before he said:

"These are peculiar words for a stranger. May I ask your name and whose interests you represent?"

His speech was quick, and had an odd halt in it, such as might be expected from one who had not conferred with his fellows for years. But there was no rudeness in its tone, nor was there any mistaking the fact that he was, both by nature and education, a gentleman. I began to take an interest in him apart from my mission.

"Mr. Felt," I replied, "my name is Tamworth. I am from Virginia, and only by chance have I become involved in a matter near to you and the man who, you tell me, is, or was, your enemy. As for the interests I represent, they are those of justice, and justice only; and it is in her behalf and for the triumph of law and righteousness that I now ask you for your confidence and such details concerning your early intercourse with Edwin Urquhart as will enable me to understand a past that will certainly yield us a clew to the present. Are you willing to give them?"

"Will I give them?" he laughed. "Will I break the seal which guards the tablets of my youth, and let a stranger's eyes read lines to which I have shut my own for these many years! Do you not know that for me to tell you what I once knew of Edwin Urquhart is to bare my own breast to view, and subject to new sufferings a heart that it has taken fifteen years of solitude to render callous?"

I gave no answer to this, only looked at him and stood waiting.

"You have hunted me out, you have touched the last string that ceases to vibrate in a man's breast—that of a wild desire for vengeance—and now you ask me—"

"To ease your memories of a burden. To drag into light the skeleton of old days, and by the light thus thrown upon it to see that it is only a skeleton, that, once beheld, should be buried and its old bones forgotten. You are too much of a man, Felt, to waste away in these wilds. Come! forget I am a stranger, and relieve yourself and me by opening these tablets you speak of, even if it does cost you a pang of the old sorrow. The talk we have had has already made a flutter in the long-closed leaves, and should I leave you this minute you could not smother the thoughts and memories to which our conversation has given rise. Then why not think to purpose and—"

He raised one hand and stopped me. The gesture was full of fire, and so was the eye he now turned away from me to gaze up at the overhanging steeps above, with their great gorges and magnificent play of light and shadow; at the valley beneath, with its broad belt of shining water winding in and out through fertile banks and growing towns, and finally at the blue dome of the sky, across which great clouds went sailing in shapes so varied and of size so majestic that it was like a vision of floating palaces on a sea of translucent azure.

Gasping in a strange mood between delight and despair, he flung up his arms.

"Ah! I have loved these hills. Of all the longings and affections that one by one have perished from my heart, the solitary passion for nature has alone remained, unlessened and undisturbed. I love these trees with their countless boughs; these rocks, with their hidden pitfalls and sudden precipices. The sky that bends above me here is bluer than any other sky; and when it frowns and gathers its storms together, and hurls them above these ledges and upon my uncovered head, I throw up my arms as I do now and exult in the tumult, and become a part of it, till the hunger in my soul is appeased, and the blood in my veins runs mildly again. And now I must quit all this. I must give to men thoughts that have been closely wedded to Nature. I must tear her image from my heart, and in her pure place substitute interests in a life I thought forever sacrificed to her worship. It is a bitter task, but I will perform it. There are other calls than those which reverberate from yon peaks. I have just heard one, and my feet go down once more into the valleys."

His arms fell with the last words, and his eyes returned again to my face.

"Come into the cave," said he. "I cannot tell my story in the sight of these pure skies."

I followed him without a word. He had affected me. The invocation in which he had indulged, and which, from another man, and other circumstances, would have struck me as a theatrical attempt upon my sympathy as forced as it was unnatural, was in him so appropriate, and in such keeping with the grandeur of the scene by which we were surrounded, that I was disarmed of criticism, and succumbed without resistance to his power.

The cave, once entered, was light enough. On the ground were spread in profusion leaves and twigs of the sweet-smelling cedar, making a carpet as pleasing as it was warm and healthful. On one side I saw a mound of the same, making a couch, across which a great cloak was spread; while beyond, the half-defined forms of a rude seat and table appeared, lending an air of habitableness to the spot, which, from the exterior, I had hardly expected to find. A long slab of stone served as a hearth, and above it I perceived a hole in the rock, toward which a thin column of smoke was rising from a few smouldering embers that yet remained burning upon the great stone below. Altogether, it was a home I had entered; and awed a little at the remembrance that it had been the refuge of this solitary man through years pregnant with events forever memorable in the history of the world as those which gave birth to a new nation, I sank down upon the pile of cedar he pointed out to me, and waited in some impatience for him to begin his tale.

This he seemed in no hurry to do. He waited so long with his chin sunk in his two hands and his eyes fixed upon vacancy, that I grew restless and was about to break the silence myself, when, without moving, he suddenly spoke.

CHAPTER VII

TWO WOMEN

"You want to hear about Edwin Urquhart. Well, you shall, but first I promise you that I shall talk much less of him than of another person. Why? because it is on account of this other person that I hate him, and solely because of this other person that I avenge myself, or seek to assist others in avenging the justice you say he has outraged.

"We were friends from boyhood. Reared in the same town and under the same influences, there was a community of interests between us that threw us together and made us what is called friends. But I never liked him. That is, I never felt a confidence in him which is essential to a mutual understanding. And, though I accepted his companionship, and was much with him at the most critical time of my life, I always kept one side, and that the better side, of my nature closed to him.

"He was a gentleman with no expectations; I the inheritor of a small fortune that made my friendship of temporary use to him, even if it did not offer him much to rely on in the future. We lived, he with an uncle who was ready to throw him off the moment he was assured that he would not marry one of his daughters, and I in my own house, which, if no manor, was at least my own, and for the present free from debt. I myself thought that Urquhart intended to marry one of the girls to whom I have just alluded. But it seems that he never meant to do this, and only encouraged his uncle to think so because he was not yet ready to give up the shelter he enjoyed with him. But of this, as I say, I was ignorant, and was consequently very much astonished when, one nightfall, in passing the great Dudleigh place, he remarked:

"'How would you like to drink a glass with me in yonder? Better than in the Fairfax kitchen, eh?'

"I thought he was joking. ''Tis a fine old house,' I observed. 'No doubt its wines are good. But it is no tavern, and I question if Miss Dudleigh would make either of us very welcome.'

"'You do! Then you don't know Miss Dudleigh,' he vaunted, with a proud swelling of his person, and a lift of his head that almost took my breath away. For, though he was a handsome fellow—too handsome for a man no worthier than he—I should no more have presumed to have associated him in my thoughts with Miss Dudleigh than if he had been a worker in her fields. Not so much because she was rich—very rich for that day and place—or that her family was an old one, and his but a mushroom stock, as that she was a being of the gentlest instincts and the purest thoughts, while he was what you may have gathered from my words—vain, coarse, cowardly and mean; an abject cur beside her, who was, and is, one of the sweetest women the sun ever shone upon."

At this expression of admiration on the part of the hermit, which proved him to be in entire ignorance of the crime which had been perpetrated against this woman, I found myself struck so aghast that I could not forbear showing it. But he was too engrossed in his reminiscences to notice my emotion, and presently continued his story by saying:

"I probably betrayed my astonishment to Urquhart, for he gave a great laugh, and forced me about toward the gates.

"'We will not be turned out,' he said. 'Let us go in and pay our respects.'

"'But,' I stammered.

"'Oh, it's all right,' he pursued. 'The fair lady is of age and has the privilege of choosing her future husband. I shall live in clover, eh? Well, it is time I lived in something. I have had a hard enough time of it so far, for a none too homely fellow.'

"I was overwhelmed; more than that, I was sickened by these words, whose import I understood only too well. Not that I had any special interest in Miss Dudleigh; indeed, I hardly knew her; but any such woman inspires respect, and I could not think of her as allied to this man without a spasm of revolt that almost amounted to fear.

"'You are going to marry her, this white rose!' I exclaimed. 'I should as soon have thought of your marrying a princess of the royal house. I hope you appreciate your unbounded good fortune.'

"He pointed to the great chimneys and imposing facade of the fine structure before us. 'Do you think I am so blind as not to know the advantage of being the master in a house like that? You must not think me quite a fool if I am not as clever a fellow as you are. Remember that I am a poorer one and like my ease better.'

"'But Miss Dudleigh?'

"'Oh, she's a trifle peaked and dull, but she's fond and not too exacting.'

"I was angry, but had no excuse for showing it. Righteous indignation he could never have understood, and to have provoked a quarrel without any definite end in view would have been folly. I remained silent, therefore, but my heart burned within me.

"It had not lost its heat when we entered her house, and when my eyes fell upon her seated at her spinet in front of a latticed window that brought out her gentle figure in all its sweet simplicity, I felt like clutching, and flinging back over the threshold, which his desecrating foot should never have crossed, the hollow-hearted being at my side, who could neither see her beauty nor estimate the worth of her innocent affection.

"There was an aunt or some such relative in the room with her, but this did not hinder the glad smile from rising to her lips as she saw us—or rather him, for she hardly seemed to notice my presence. I learned afterward that this aunt had been greatly instrumental in bringing these incongruous natures together; that for reasons of her own, which I have never attempted to fathom, she thought Edwin Urquhart the best husband that her niece could have, and not only introduced him into the house, but stood so much his friend during the first days of his courtship that she gradually imparted to her niece her own enthusiasm, till the poor girl saw—or thought she saw—the ideal of her dreams in the base and shallow being whom I called my friend.

"However that may be, she certainly rose from her spinet that night in a pretty confusion that made her absolutely lovely, and advancing with the mingled dignity of the heiress and the tender bashfulness of the maiden in the presence of him she loved, she tendered us a courtesy whose grace put me out of ease with myself, so much it expressed the manners of people removed from the sphere in which it had hitherto been my lot to move.

"But Urquhart showed no embarrassment. His fine figure—he had that—bent forward with the most courtly of bows, and after the introduction of my humble self to her notice, he entered into a conversation which, if shallow, was at least bright, and for the moment interesting. As I had no wish to talk, I gave myself up to watching her, and came away at last more fixed than ever in my belief of her extreme worthiness and of his extreme presumption in thinking of calling so perfect a creature his.

"'Would to God she was as poor as Janet Fairfax,' I thought to myself. 'Then she would never have attracted his attention, and might have known what happiness was with some man who could appreciate her. Now she is doomed, and being fatherless and motherless, will rush on to her fate, and no one can stop her.'

"Thus I thought, and thus I continued to think as chance and Urquhart's stubborn will led me more and more to her house, and within the radius of her gentle influence. But my thoughts never went further. I never saw her, even in my dreams, fostered by me, or soothed of an old grief by my love and affection. For though she was a dainty and gracious being, with beauty enough to delight the eyes and warm the heart, she was not the one destined to move me, and awake the tumultuous passions that lay dormant in my own scarcely understood nature. Urquhart, therefore, was not acting unwisely in taking me there so often, though, if I could have foreseen what was likely to be the result of those visits, I should have leaped from my house's roof on to the stones below before I had passed again under those fatal portals.

"And yet—would I? Do we fear suffering or apathy most? Is it from experience or the monotony of a commonplace existence that we quickest flee? A man with passions like mine must love; and if that love comes girt with flame and mysterious death, he still must embrace it, and rise and fall as the destinies will.

"But I talk riddles. I have not yet told you of her; and yet speak of fire and death. I will try to be more coherent, if only to show that the years have brought me some mastery over myself. One day—it was a fall day and beautiful as limpid sunshine and a world of yellowing woods could make it—I went to Miss Dudleigh's house to apologize for my friend, who had wished to improve the gorgeous sunshine elsewhere.

"I had by this time lost all fear of her, as well as of her rich and spacious surroundings, and passed through the hospitable door and along the wide halls to the especial room in which we were wont to find her, with that freedom engendered by an intimacy as cordial as it was sincere. It was the room where first I had seen her, the room with the wide latticed window at the back, and the spinet beneath it, and the old carven chair of oak in which her white-clad form had always looked so ethereal; and I entered it smiling, expecting to see her delicate figure rise from the window, and advance toward me with that look of surprise and possible disappointment which the absence of Urquhart would be apt to arouse in this too loving nature. But the room was empty and the spinet closed, and I was about turning to find a servant, when I felt an influence stealing over me so subtle and so peculiar that I stood petrified and enthralled, hardly knowing if it were music that held me spell-bound or some unknown and subduing perfume, that, filling my senses, worked upon my brain, and made me feel like a man transported at a breath from the land of reality into a land of dreams.

"So potent the spell, so inexplicable its action, that minutes may have elapsed before I wrenched myself free from its power and looked to see what it was that so moved me. When I did, I found myself at a loss to explain it. Whether it was music or perfume, or just the emanation from an intense personality, I have never determined. I only know that when I turned, I saw standing before me, in an attitude of waiting, a woman of such marvelous attractions, and yet of an order of beauty so bizarre and out of keeping with the times and the place in which she stood, that I forgot to question everything but my own sanity and the reality of a vision so unprecedented in all my experience. I therefore simply stood like her, speechless and lost, and only came to myself when the figure before me suddenly melted from a statue into a woman, and, with a deep and graceful courtesy, almost daring in its abandonment, said:

"'You must be Master Felt, I take it. Master Urquhart would never be so thrown off his balance by a simple girl like me.'

"There are voices that pierce like arrows and sink deep into the heart, which closes over their sweetness forever. So it was with this voice. From its first sound to its last it held me enthralled, and had she shown but half the beauty she did, those accents of hers would have made me her slave. As it was, I was more than her slave. I instantly became all and everything to her. I breathed but as she breathed, and in the absorbing delight which from that moment took hold of me I lost all sense of the proprieties and conventionalities of social intercourse, and only thought of drinking in at one draught the strange and mysterious loveliness which I saw revealed before me.

"She was not a tall woman, no taller than Miss Dudleigh. Nor was she of marked carriage or build. Her form, indeed, seemed only made to express suppleness and passion, and was as speaking in its slight proportions as if it had breathed forth the nobler attributes of majesty and strength. Her dress was dark, and clung to every curve with a loving persistence bewildering in its effect upon an eye like mine. Upon the bust, and just below the white throat, burned a mass of gorgeous flowers as ruddy as wine; and from one delicate hand a long vine trailed to the floor. But it was in her face that her power lay; in her eyes possibly, though I scarcely think so, for there were curves to her lips such as I have never seen in any other, and a delicate turn to her nostril that at times made me feel as if she were breathing fire. Her skin was pale, her forehead broad and low, her nose straight, and her lips of a brilliant vermilion. I, however, saw only her eyes, though I may have been influenced by the rest of her bewildering physiognomy; they were so large, so changeful, so full of alternating flames and languor, so indeterminate in color, and yet so persistent in their effect upon the eye and the feelings. Looking at them, I swore she was an anomaly. Gazing into them, I resolved that she was this only because she let herself be natural and sought to smother none of the fires which had been enkindled by a bountiful nature within her soul.

"While I was reasoning thus, she made me another mock courtesy, and explaining her presence by saying she was a cousin of Miss Dudleigh's, ventured to remark that, if Master Felt would be kind enough to state his errand, she would be glad to carry it to Miss Dudleigh. I answered confusedly, but with a fervor she could not fail to understand, and following up this effort by another, led her into a conversation in which my responses gradually became such as she should expect from a gentleman and an equal.

"For with her, notwithstanding her beauty, and the sense of splendor and luxury which breathed from her mysterious presence, I never felt that sense of personal inferiority I experienced at first with Miss Dudleigh. Whether I recognized then, as now, the lack of those high qualities which lift one mortal above another, I do not know. I am only certain that, while I regarded her as a woman to be obeyed, to be loved, to be followed through life, through death, into whatsoever regions of horror, danger, and pain she might lead me, I never looked upon her as a being out of my world or beyond my reach, except so far as her caprice might carry her.

"It was therefore with the fixed determination to force from her some of the interest she had awakened in me, that I grasped at this first opportunity of conversation; and in spite of her unrest—she did not want to linger—held her to the spot till I had made her feel that a man had come into her life whose will meant something, and to whom, if she did not subdue the light of her glances, she must give account for every added throb she caused to beat in his proud heart.

"This done I let her go, for Miss Dudleigh was not well and needed her, and the door closed behind her mysterious smile, and the sound of her steps died out in the hall, and in fancy only could I behold her supple, dark-clad form go up the broad staircase, projecting itself now against the golden daylight falling through one window, and now against the clustering vines that screened another, till she disappeared in regions of which I knew nothing and whither even my daring imagination presumed not to follow. And the vision never left my eyes nor her form my heart, and I went out in my turn, a burning, eager, determined man, where in a short half hour before I had entered cold and self-satisfied, without hope and without exaltation.

"This was the beginning. In a week the earth and sky held nothing for me but that woman. Her name, which I had not learned at our first interview, was Marah Leighton—a fitting watch-word for a struggle that could terminate only with my life! For I had got to the pass that this woman must be mine. I would have her for my wife or see her dead; she should never leave the town with another. Yes; homely as I was, without recommendation of family, or more means than enough to keep a wife from want, I boldly entered upon this determination, and in the face of some dozen lovers, that at the first revelation of her beauty began to swarm about her steps, pressed my claims and pushed forward my suit till I finally gained a hearing, and after that a promise, which, if vague, was more than any of her other lovers could boast of, or why did they all gradually withdraw from the struggle, leaving me alone in my homage?

"The uncertainties of her position (she was an orphan and dependent upon Miss Dudleigh for subsistence) had added greatly to my tenderness for her. It also added to my hope. For if I were poor, she was poorer, and ought to find in the managing of my humble home a satisfaction she could not experience in the enjoyment of a relative's bounty, even if that relative was a woman like Honora Dudleigh. And yet one doubts an exultant happiness; and as I grew to know her better, I realized that if I ever did succeed in making her mine, I must see to it that my fortunes bettered, as she would never be happy as a poor man's wife, even if that man brought her independence and love.

"She loved splendor, she loved distinction, she loved the frivolities of life. Not with a childish pleasure or even a girlish enthusiasm, but with a woman's strong and determined spirit. I have seen her pace through and through those great halls just for the pleasure of realizing their spaciousness; and though the sight made my heart cringe, I have admired her step and the poise of her head as much as if she had been the queen of it all, and I her humblest vassal. Then her luxury! It showed as plainly in her poverty as it could have done in wealth. If it were flowers she handled, it was as a goddess would handle them. None were too beautiful, or too costly, or too rare for her restless fingers to pluck, or her dainty feet to tread on. Had she possessed jewels, she would have worn them like roses, and flung them away almost as freely if they had displeased her or she had grown weary of them. Love was to her a jewel, and she wore it just now because it suited her fancy to do so; but would not the day come when she would grow tired of it or demand another, and so fling it and me to the dogs?

"I did not ask. I was permitted to walk at her side, and pay her my court, and now and then, when the humor took her, to press her hand or drop a kiss upon the rosy palm; and while I could do this, was it for me to question a future which seemed more likely to hold fewer pleasures than more?

"But I grow diffuse; I must return to facts. Honora Dudleigh, who saw my devotion, encouraged it. I wondered at it sometimes, for she knew the smallness of my fortune, and must have known the nature of the woman I expected to share it. But as time passed I wondered less, for her woman's intuition must have told her, what observation had as yet failed to tell me, that there was trouble in the air, and that Marah needed a protector.

"The day that I first recognized this fact made an era in my life. I had been so happy, so at ease with myself, so sure of her growing confidence and of my coming happiness. That I had cause for this, the conduct of her friends and the jealousy of her lovers seemed to prove. Though she gave no visible token of her regard, she clung to me as to a support, and allowed my passion the constant feast of her presence and the stimulation of her voice.

"Her enchantments, and they were innumerable, were never spared me, nor did she stint herself of a smile that could allure, nor of a glance that could arouse or perplex.

"I was happy, and questioned only the extent of my patience, which I felt fast giving way as the preparations for Miss Dudleigh's marriage proceeded without my seeing any immediate prospect of my own. You can realize, then, the maddening nature of the shock which I received when, coming quietly into the house as I did one day, I beheld her face disappearing through one of the doorways, with that look upon it which I had always felt was natural to it, but which no passion of mine had ever been able to evoke, and then perceived in the shadow from which she had just glided, Edwin Urquhart, pale as excessive feeling could make him, and so shaken by the first real emotion which had ever probably moved his selfish soul that he not only failed to see me when I advanced, but hastened by me, and away into the solitudes of the garden, without noticing my existence, or honoring with a reply the words of wrath and confusion which, in my misery and despair, I threw after him."

CHAPTER VIII

A SUDDEN BETROTHAL

"As for myself," continued Mark Felt, "I stood crushed, and after the first torrent of emotion had swept by, lifted my head like a drowning man and looked wildly about, as if, in the catastrophe which overwhelmed me, all nature must have changed, and I should find myself in a strange place. The sight of the door through which Marah Leighton had passed stung me into tortured existence again. With a roar of passion and hate I sprang toward it, burst it open, and passed in. Instantly silence and semi-darkness fell upon me, through which I felt her presence exhaling its wonted perfume, though I could see nothing but the dim shapes of unaccustomed articles of furniture grouped against a window that was almost completely closed from the light of day.

"Advancing, I gazed upon chair after chair. They were all empty, and not till I reached the further corner did I find her, thrown at full length upon a couch, with her head buried in her arms, and motionless as any stone. Confused, appalled even, for I had never seen her otherwise than erect and mocking, I stumbled back, and would have fled, but that she suddenly arose, and flinging back her head, gave me one look, which I felt rather than saw, and bursting into a peal of laughter, called me to account for disturbing the first minute of rest she had known that day.

"I was dumbounded. If she had consulted all her wiles, and sought for the one best way to silence me, she could not have chanced on one surer than this. I gazed at her quite helpless, and forgot—actually forgot—what had drawn me into her presence, and only asked to get a good glimpse of her face, which, in the dim light, was more like that of a spirit than of a woman—a mocking spirit, in whom no love could lodge, whatever my fancy might have pictured in the delirium of the moment that had just passed.

"She seemed to comprehend my mood, for she flung back the curtain and drew herself up to her full height before me.

"'Did you think I was playing the coquette?' she asked. 'Well, perhaps I was; women like me must have their amusements; but—'

"Oh! the languishment in that but. I shut my eyes as I heard it. I could neither bear its sound, nor the sight of her face.

"'You listened to him. He was making love to you—he, the promised husband of another; and you—'

"She forced me to open my eyes.

"'And I?' she repeated, with an indescribable emphasis that called up the blushes to my cheek.

"'And you,' I went on, answering her demand without hesitation, 'the beloved of an honest man who would die to keep you true, and will die if you play him false!'

"She sighed. Softness took the place of scorn; she involuntarily held out her hand.

"I was amazed; she had never done so much before. I seized that hand, I pressed it wildly, hungrily, and with lingering fondness.

"'Do you not know that you are everything to me?' I asked. 'That to win you I am ready to do everything, barter anything, suffer anything but shame! You are my fate, Marah; will you not let me be yours?'

"She was silent; she had drawn her hand from mine and had locked it in its fellow, and now stood with them hanging down before her, fixed as a statue, in a reverie I could neither fathom nor break.

"'You are beautiful,' I went on, 'too beautiful for me; but I love you. You are proud, also, and would grace the noblest palaces of the old world; but they are far away, and my home is near and eager to welcome you. You are dainty and have never taught your hands to toil, or your feet to walk our common earth; but there are affections that sweeten labor, and under my roof you will be so honored, so aided and so beloved, that you will soon learn there are pleasures of the fireside that can compensate for its cares, and triumphs of the affections that are beyond the dignities of outside life.'

"Her lip curled and her hands parted. She lifted one rosy palm and looked at it, then she glanced at me.

"'I shall never work,' she said.

"My heart contracted, but I could not give her up. Madness as it was to put faith and life in the grasp of such a woman, I was too little of a man or too much of a one to turn my back upon a hope which, even in its realization, could bring me nothing but pain.

"'You shall not work,' I declared. And I meant it. If I died she should not handle anything harsher than rose leaves in her new home.

"'You want me?' She breathed it. I stood in a gasp of hope and fear.

"'More than I want heaven! Or, rather, you are my heaven.'

"'We will be married before Honora,' she murmured. And gliding from my side before I had recovered from the shock of a promise so unexpected, a bliss so unforeseen and immediate, she vanished from my sight, and nothing but the perfume which lingered behind her remained to tell me that it was not all a dream, and I the most presumptuous being alive.

"And so the hour that opened in disaster ended in joy; and from the heart of what I deemed an irredeemable disaster rose a hope that for several days put wings to my feet. Then something began to tarnish my delight, an impalpable dread seized me, and though I worked with love and fury upon my house, which I had begun adorning for my bride, I began to question if she had played the coquette in smiling upon Edwin Urquhart, and whether in the mockery of the laugh with which she had dismissed my accusations there had not been some regret for a love she dared not entertain, but yet suffered to lose. The memory of the glow in her eyes, as she turned away from him at my step, returned with growing power, and I decided that if this were coquetry, it were sweeter than love, and longed to ask her to play the coquette with me. But she never did, and though she did not smile upon him again in my presence, I felt that her beauty was more bewildering, her voice more enchanting, when he was in the room with us than when chance or my purpose found us alone. To settle my doubts, I left watching her and began to watch him, and when I found that he betrayed nothing, I turned my attention from them both and bestowed it upon Miss Dudleigh."

CHAPTER IX

MARAH

"Great heaven! why had I not noticed Miss Dudleigh before! In her changed face, and in the wasting of her delicate form, I saw that my fears were not all vain, inasmuch as they were shared by her; and shocked at evidences so much beyond my expectations, I knew not whether to shed the bitter tears which rose to my eyes in pity for her or in rage for myself.

"We were sitting all together, and I had a full opportunity to observe the mournful smile that now and then crossed her lips as Marah uttered some brighter sally than common or broke—as she often did—into song that rippled for a minute through the heavy air and then ceased as suddenly as it had begun. She looked much oftener at Marah than at Urquhart, and seemed to be asking in what lay the charm that subdued everybody, even herself. And when she seemed to receive no answer to her secret questioning, her eyes fell and a sigh stirred her lips, which, if unheard by the preoccupied man at her side, rang on in my ears long after I had bidden farewell to her and the siren whose smiles, intentionally or unintentionally, seemed destined to bring shipwreck into three lives.

"It was not the last time I heard that sigh. As the weeks progressed it fluttered oftener and oftener from between those pale lips, and at last the change in Miss Dudleigh became so marked that people stopped in the midst of their talk about the stamp act to remark upon Miss Dudleigh's growing weakness, and venture assertions that she would never live to be a bride. And yet the preparations for her bridal and for mine went on, and the day set apart for the latter drew bewilderingly near.

"Marah saw my perplexity and her cousin's grief, but did nothing to dispel the one or assuage the other. She seemed to be too busy. She was embroidering a famous stomacher for herself, and while a sprig of it remained unworked she had neither eyes nor attention for anything else, even for the bleeding hearts around her. She would smile—O yes, smile upon me, smile upon Honora, and not smile upon him; but she would not meet her cousin's true eyes, nor would she grant me one minute apart from the rest in which I could utter my fears or demand the breaking of that spell whose effects were so visible, even if its workings were secret and imperceptible. But at last the stomacher was finished, and as it dropped from her hands I threw myself at her feet, and from this position, looking into her eyes, I whispered:

"'This is the last thing that shall ever flaunt itself between us. You are to be mine now, and in token of your truth come with me into the conservatory, for I have words to utter that will not be put off.'

"'You are cruel,' she murmured, 'you are tyrannical. This is a time of revolt; shall I revolt, too?'

"Maddened, for her eyes were not looking at me, but at him, I leaped to my feet, and, regardless of everything but my determination to end this uncertainty then and there, I lifted her and carried her out of the room into another, where I could have her alone, and without the humiliating sense of his presence.

"My bold act seemed to frighten her, for she stood very still where I had placed her, only trembling slightly when I looked at her and cried:

"'Did you ask that question of me? Am I to understand you want to break your fetters?'

"She plucked a rose from her breast and crumpled it to atoms between her hands.

"'O why are they not golden ones!' she asked. 'I am miserable because we must be poor; because—because I want to ride in a carriage, because I want to wear jewels and own a dozen servants, and trample on the pride of women plainer than myself. I hate your humble home, I hate your stiff Dutch kitchen, I hate your sordid ways and the decent respectability that is all you can offer me. Were you beautiful as Adonis, it would make no difference. I was born to drink wine and not water, and I shall never forgive you for forcing me to take your crystal goblet in my hands, while, if I had waited—'

"She stopped, panting. I let my whole pent-up jealousy out in a word.

"'Edwin Urquhart has not even a crystal goblet to offer you. He is poorer than I am, and will remain so till he has actually married Miss Dudleigh.'

"'Don't I know it!' she flashed out. 'If it had been otherwise do you think—'

"She had the grace or the wisdom to falter. I regret it now. I regret that she did not go on and reveal her whole soul to me in one fell burst of feeling. As it was, I trembled with jealousy and passion, but I did not cast her from me.

"'Then you acknowledge—' I cried.

"But she would acknowledge nothing. 'I love no one,' she asserted, 'no one. I want what I want, but none of you can give it to me.'

"Then blame me as you will, I took a great resolve. I determined to give her what she craved; convinced of her sordid nature, convinced of her heartlessness and the folly of ever thinking she could even understand, much less reciprocate my passion, I was so much under her sway at that moment that I would have flung at her feet kingdoms had I possessed them. Flushing, I seized her hand.

"'You do not know what a man in love can do,' I cried. 'Trust me; give me yourself as you have promised, and sooner or later I will give you what you have asked. I am not a weak man or an incompetent one. Politics opens a vast field to an ambitious nature, and if war breaks out, as we all expect it will, you will see me rise to the front, if I have you for my wife and inspiration.'

"The scorn in her eyes did not abate. 'O you men!' she cried. 'You think you give us everything with a promise. A war! What is the history of wars? Demolished homes, broken fortunes, rack, ruin and desolation. Is there gold, or honor, or ease in these? A war! It will not be a war. It will be a struggle in which men will fight barefoot and on empty stomachs for the privilege of calling themselves free. I have no sympathy with such a war. It robs us of comfort in the present and brings nothing worth waiting for in the future. Were I to have my will, I would take the arm of the first officer returning to England and remain there. I hate this country, so new, so crude, so democratic! I should like to live where I could ride over the necks of common people.'

"A tory and an aristocrat! Another gulf between us. I looked at her in horror, but, alas! the horror was strangely mixed with admiration. She was such a burning embodiment of pride. Her peculiar beauty—the source of which I have never to this day been able to fathom—lent itself so readily to the expression of fury and disdain, that, recoil as I would from her principles, I could not shut my eyes to the fascination of her glance or the torturing charm that hid in the corners of her pouting lips. She was a queen. Oh, yes, but the queen of some strange realm in a distant oriental land, where right and wrong were only words, and the sole end of beauty was delight, without reference to God or one's fellows. I saw it all, I felt it all, yet I lingered. She was to be my wife in three days, and the intoxication of this prospect was in my blood and brain.

"'You will do so and so,' were her next words. 'You will give me what I ask when you have won it. But I cannot wait for the winning; I want it now. Do you know what I would do to get the wealth I was born to? I would risk life! I would walk on burning plowshares! I would—'

"She stopped, and I saw the lines come out in her forehead. She was thinking—thinking deeply. I felt the shadow of a great horror creeping over me. I caught her impetuously in my arms. I kissed her passionately to drive away the demons. I begged and implored her to forget her evil thoughts, and be the woman I could love and cherish; and finally I moved her. She shook herself free, but she also shook the shadow from her brow. She even found a smile to bestow upon me; and was it a tear? Could it have been a tear I saw for a moment glisten in her eye as she turned half petulantly, half imperiously away? I have never known, but the very suspicion filled my heart to overflowing, and the great sobs rose in my breast; and—fool that I was—I was about to beg her pardon, when she gave me one other look, and I merely faltered out:

"'Where will you find another love like mine, Marah? If you got your gold, you would soon miss something which only comes with love. You would be unhappy, and curse the day you left my arms. I am your master, Marah; why not make me a happy one?'

"'I expect,' she murmured, 'to marry you.'

"'And then?' I could not help it; the words sprang to my lips involuntarily.

"Her eyes opened wide; she literally flashed them upon me. I felt their lightnings play all about my doubtful nature, and scorch it.

"'I will be your wife,' she uttered gravely.

"I fell at her feet. I kissed the hem of her robe. In that moment I adored her. 'O best and fairest!' I cried, 'I will make you happy. I will fill your hopes to the full. You shall ride in a carriage, and your will shall be a law to those who smile in scorn upon you now, and you will be—'

"'Mistress Felt, of most honorable degree,' she finished, with the half laughing disdain she could never keep long out of her words.

"And thus I became again her slave, and lived in that sweet, if servile, condition till the hour of our nuptials came, and I went to conduct her to the church where, in sight of half the town, she was to be made my wife. Shall I ever forget that morning? It was a December day, but the heavens were blue and the earth white, and not a cloud bespoke a rising storm. As for me, I walked on air, all the more that I knew Urquhart was out of town and would not be present at the wedding. He had gone away on some behest of Miss Dudleigh's immediately after the last interview I have mentioned, and would not come back, or so I had been told, till after Miss Leighton had been Mistress Felt for a week. So there was nothing to mar my day or make my entrance into Miss Dudleigh's house anything but one of promise. I saw Miss Dudleigh first. She was standing in the vast colonial hall when I entered, and in her gala robes, and with the sunshine on her head, she looked almost happy. Yet she was greatly changed from her old self, and I felt much like pouring out my soul to her and bidding her to break a tie that would never bring her peace, or even honor. But I feared to shatter my own hopes. Selfish being that I was, I dreaded to have her made free, lest— What? My thoughts did not interpret my fears, for at that moment a sunbeam struck down the stairs and through my heart, and, looking up, I saw Marah descending, and thought and reason flew to greet her.

"She had been robed by her cousin's bounteous hand, and her dress of stiff yellow brocade burned in the morning light with almost as much brilliance as the sunshine itself. Folded across her bust was the wonderful stomacher, under whose making I had suffered so many emotions that each sprig of work upon it seemed to have its own tale of misery for my eyes, and fixed against this and her white throat were those masses of flowers without which her beauty never seemed quite complete. In her hair, which was piled high above her forehead, flashed a huge golden comb, and upon her arm gleamed two bracelets, whose exquisite workmanship was well known to me, for they had been an heirloom in my family for years. She was fair as a dream, proud as a queen, cold as a statue, but she was mine! Was not the minister waiting for us at the church? and were not the horses that were to take us there even now champing their bits before the door?

"She rode with me. Four white horses had been attached to Miss Dudleigh's coach, and behind these we passed in state out through the noble park that separated this lordly house from the rest, into the closely packed streets, where hundreds waited to catch a glimpse of the most beautiful woman in Albany, going to be made a bride.

"Miss Dudleigh rode behind us in another coach, and the murmur which greeted our appearance did not die out till after she had passed, for they knew she would soon be riding the same road with even greater state, if not with so much beauty; and the people of Albany loved Honora Dudleigh, for she was ever a beneficent spirit to them, and more than ever, since a shadow had fallen upon her happiness, and she had come to know what misery was.

"And thus we passed on, Marah with a glowing flush of triumph burning on her cheek and I in one of those moods of happiness whose rapture was so unalloyed that I scarcely heard the half-laughing comments of those who saw with wonder how plain was the man who had succeeded in carrying off this well-known beauty. And the greater part of the way was traversed, and the bells of the old North Church became audible, and in a moment more we should have seen the belfry of the church itself rising before us, when, suddenly, the woman that I loved, the woman whose nuptials the minister was waiting to celebrate, gave a great start, and, turning quickly toward me, cried:

"'Turn the horses' heads! I do not go to the church with you to-day. Not if you kill me, Mark Felt!'

"You have heard of stray bullets coming singing from some unknown quarter and striking a person seated at a feast. Such a bullet struck me then. I looked at her in horror."

CHAPTER X

AT THE FOOT OF THE STAIRS

"'You think I am playing with you,' she murmured. 'I am not. I have sickened of these nuptials and am going back. If you want to, you may kill me where I sit. You carry a dagger, I know; one more red blossom will not show on my breast. Give it to me if you will, but turn the horses.'

"She meant it, however much my lost heart might cry out for its happiness and honor. Leaning forward, I told the pompous driver that Miss Leighton had been taken very ill, and bade him drive back; and then with the calmness born of utter despair and loss, I said to her:

"'In pity for my pride drop your head upon my shoulder. I have said you were sick, and sick you must be. It is the least you can do for me now.'

"She obeyed me. That head on which in fancy I had set the crowns of empires, for whose every hair my heart had given a throb, sank coldly down till it rested upon the heart she had broken; and while I steadied my nerves to meet the changed faces of the crowd, the carriage gave a sudden turn, and amid murmurings that fell almost unheeded on my benumbed senses, we wheeled about and faced again the gates through which we had so lately issued.

"'She is ill,' I shouted to Miss Dudleigh, as we passed her carriage. But she gave me no reply. She was gazing over the heads of the crowd at some distant object that enthralled her every look and sense; and moved by her expression as I thought never to be moved by anything again, I followed her glance, and there, on the outskirts of the crowd, crouching amid branches that yet refused to hide him, I saw Edwin Urquhart; and the miserable truth smote home to my heart that it was he who had stopped my marriage—he, whom I had thought far distant, but who had now come to hinder, by some secret gesture or glance, my bride on her path to the altar.

"A dagger was hidden in my breast, and I still wonder that I did not leap from the carriage, burst through the crowd, and slay him where he crouched in cowardly ambush. But I let the moment go by, perhaps because I dreaded to bring the shadow of another woe into Miss Dudleigh's white face, and almost immediately the throng had surged in thickly between us, and Miss Dudleigh's carriage had turned after ours, and there was nothing further to do but to ride back, with the false face pressed in seeming insensibility to my breast, and that false heart beating out its cold throbs of triumph upon mine.

"I bore it, glancing down but once upon her. Had the ride before me been one of miles I should have gone on in the same mechanical way, for my very being was petrified. Rage, fear, sorrow and despair, all seemed like dreams to me. I wondered that I had ever felt anything, and stared on and on at the blue sky before me, conscious of but one haunting thought that repeated itself again and again in my brain— that her power lay not in her eyes, as I had always been assured, but in those strange curves about her mouth. For her eyes were closed now, and yet I was coldly conscious of the fact that she had never looked more beautiful or more fitted to move a man, if a man had any heart left to be moved.

"The stopping of the carriage before the great door of Miss Dudleigh's house roused me to the necessity for action.

"'I must carry you in,' I whispered. 'I beg your pardon for it, but it is necessary to the farce.' And following up my words by action, I lifted her from the seat, cold and unresponsive as a stone, and carried her into the house and set her down before the astonished eyes of such servants as had remained to guard the house in our absence.

"'Miss Leighton has not been married,' I cried. 'She was taken ill on the way to church, and I have brought her back. She needs no attendance.' And I waved them all back, for their startled, gaping countenances infuriated me, and threatened to shatter the dreadful calmness which was my only strength.

"As they disappeared, murmuring and peering, Miss Dudleigh entered. I gave her one glance and dropped my eyes. She and I could not bear each other's looks yet. Meantime Marah stood erect in the center of the hall, her face pale, her lips set, her eyes fixed upon vacancy. Not a word passed our three mouths. At last a petulant murmur broke the dreadful silence, and Marah, tossing her head in disdain, turned away before our eyes and began to mount the stairs.

"I felt my blood, which for many minutes had seemed at a standstill, pour with a rush through vein and artery, and darting to her side, I caught her by the hand and held her to her place.

"'You shall not go up,' I cried, 'till you and I have understood each other. You have refused to marry me to-day. Was it some caprice that moved you, or—' I paused and looked behind me; Miss Dudleigh had shrunk from sight into one of the rooms—'or because you saw Edwin Urquhart in the crowd and followed his commanding gesture?'

"The hand which I held grew cold as ice. She drew it away and looked at me haughtily, but I saw that I had frightened her.

"'Edwin Urquhart is nothing to me,' came in low but emphatic tones from her lips. 'I did not want to marry any one, and I said so. It would be better if more brides hesitated on the threshold of matrimony instead of crossing it to their ruin.'

"I could have killed her, but I subdued myself. I knew that I had lost her; that in another moment she would be gone, never to enter my presence again as my promised wife; but I uttered no word, honored her with no glance; merely made her a low bow and stepped back, as I thought, master of myself again.

"But in that final instant one last arrow entered my breast, and darting back to her side, I whispered, in what must have been a terrible voice:

"'Go, falsest of the false! I have done with you! But if you have lied to me—if you think to trip up Edwin Urquhart in his duty, and break Honora Dudleigh's noble heart, and shame my honor—I will kill you as I would a snake in the grass! You shall never approach the altar with another as nearly as you have this day with me!'

"And with the last mockery of a look, in which every detail of her beauty flashed with almost an unbearable insistence upon my eyes, I turned my back upon her and strode toward the outer door."

CHAPTER XI

HONORA

"But I did not pass it. A sound struck my ear. It was that of a smothered sob, and it came from the room where I had first seen Miss Dudleigh. Instantly a vision of that sweet form bowed in misery struck upon my still palpitating heart; and moved at a grief I knew to be well nigh as bitter as my own, I stopped before the half-closed door, and gently pushed it open.

"Miss Dudleigh at once advanced to meet me. Tears were on her cheeks, but she walked very firmly, and took my hand with an inquiry in her soft eyes that almost drove me distracted.

"'What shall I do?' I cried to myself. 'Tell this woman to beware, or leave her to fight her battles alone?' No answer came from my inmost soul. I was appalled by her weakness and my own selfishness, and bowed my head and said nothing.

"'A strange ending to the hopes of this day,' were the words that thereupon fell from her lips. 'Is—is—Marah ill, or did one of her strange moods overtake her?'

"'I do not understand Miss Leighton,' I replied. 'The time I have spent in the study of her character has been wasted. I shall never undertake to open the book again.'

"'Then,' she faltered, and an absolute terror grew in her eyes, 'you are going to leave her. She is going to be free, and—' The white cheeks grew scarlet. She evidently feared that she had shown me her heart.

"Affected, but irresolute still, I took her hand and carried it to my lips.

"'Let me thank you,' said I, 'for glimpses into a nature so noble and womanly that I am saved in this hour from cursing all womankind.'

"Ah, how she sighed.

"'You are good,' she murmured. 'You have deserved a better fate. But it is the lot of goodness and truth ever to meet with misappreciation and disdain. Here, here, only,' and she struck her breast with her clenched right hand, 'lie the rewards for honesty, long-suffering, and tenderness. In the world without there is nothing.'

"Tears, which I could not restrain, welled up to my eyes. I could never have wept for my own suffering, but for hers it seemed both natural and real. Ah, why had she thrown the treasures of her heart away upon a fool? Why had she given the trust of her heart to a villain? I opened my lips to speak; she saw his name faltering on my tongue, and stopped me.

"'Don't!' she breathed. 'I know what you would say and I cannot bear it. I was motherless, fatherless, almost friendless, and I relied upon the wisdom of an aunt, whose judgment was, perhaps, not all that it should have been. But it is too late now for regrets. I have launched my boat, and it must sail on; only— you are an honest man and will respect my confidence—was it Mr. Urquhart I saw on the outskirts of the crowd to-day?'

"I bowed. I knew she had not asked because she had any doubts as to the fact of his being there, but because she wanted to see if I had recognized him and owed any of my misery to that fact.

"'It was he,' said I, and said no more.

"The mask fell from her countenance. She clasped her hands together till they showed white as marble.

"'Oh! we are four miserable ones!' she cried. 'He—'

"It was my turn to stop her.

"'I would rather you did not say it,' I exclaimed. 'I can bear much, but not to hear another person utter words that will force me to think of the dagger I carry always in my breast. Besides, we may be mistaken.' I did not believe it, but I forced myself to say it. 'She declares he is nothing to her, and if that is so, you might wish to have kept silent.'

"'She says! Ah! can you believe her? do you?'

"'I must—or go mad.'

"'Then I will believe her, too. I am so slightly tied to this world that has deceived me, that I will trust on a little while longer, even if my trust lands me in my grave. I had rather die than discover deceit where I had looked for honesty and gratitude.'

"I was a coward, perhaps, but I did not try to dissuade her. Though she was fatherless and motherless, and loverless and friendless, I let her grasp at this wisp of hope and cling to it, though I knew it would never hold, and that her only chance for happiness was passing from her.

"'If he were not poor,' she now breathed rather than whispered, 'I would find it easier to rend myself free. But he has nothing but what lies in my future, and if I should make a mistake and do injustice to a man that is merely suffering under a temporary intoxication, I should rob him of his only hope, without adding one chance to my own.'

"I bowed, and made a movement toward the door. I could not stand much more of this strain.

"'You are going?' she cried. 'Well, I cannot keep you. But that dagger! You will promise me to throw it away? You do not need it in defense, and you do not want to kill me before my time.'

"No, no; I did not want to kill her. Grief was doing that fast enough; so I thought at that time. Shuddering, but resolute, I drew the tiny steel from my breast and laid it in her hand.

"'It is all I can give you to show you my appreciation of your goodness.' And not trusting myself to linger longer lest I should take it again from her hand, I went out and walked hastily from the house.

"If you asked me what road I took, or through what streets I passed, or whose eye I encountered in my next hour's walking through the town, I could not tell you. If jeers followed me, I heard them not; if I was the recipient of sympathizing looks and wondering conjectures, they were all lost upon eyes that were blind and ears that were deaf. I did not even feel; and did not realize till night that I had been wandering for hours without my cloak, which I had left in the carriage and forgotten to take again when I went out. The first knowledge I had of my surroundings was when I found an obstruction in my path, and looking up, saw myself in front of my own door, and not two feet from me, Edwin Urquhart."

CHAPTER XII

EDWIN URQUHART

In that moment Mark Felt paused and cast a glance toward the Hudson far below us. Then he resumed his narrative.

"I drew back," he said, "and clenched my hands to keep myself from strangling Urquhart. Then I broke into hurried pants, that subsided gradually into words of perplexity and amazement as I met his eye, and realized that it contained nothing but a rude sort of sympathy and good fellowship.

"'How? Why? What do you mean by coming back?' I cried. 'You said you would be gone a week. You swore—'

"A gay laugh interrupted me.

"'And must a man keep every oath he makes, especially when it separates him from a charming betrothed, and a friend who swore that he would make this day his wedding one?'

"'Urquhart!'

"'Felt!'

"'Are you a monster or are you—'

"'A self-possessed man who is going to take in charge a crazy one. Come into the house, Mark, a dozen eyes can see us here.'

"He took me in charge; he piloted me into my own dwelling—he whose whole body I had always esteemed weaker than my little finger; my enemy too, or so I considered him; the cause of half my grief, of all my shame, the beginning and end of my hatreds.

"When we were closeted, as we soon were in the room I had expended so much upon to make worthy of my bride, he came and stood before me and uttered these unexpected words:

"'Felt, I like you. You are the only friend I have, and I am indebted to you. Now, what have you against me?'

"I was astonished. His whole look and bearing were so different from what I had expected, so different from anything I had ever seen in him before. I began to question my doubts, and dropped my eyes as he pursued:

"'You have been disappointed in your marriage, I hear; but that need not make you as downcast as this. A woman as capricious as Miss Leighton might easily imagine she was too ill to go through the ceremony to-day. But she must have repented of her folly by this time, and in a week will reward you as your patience deserves. But what have I got to do with it? For incredible as it appears, your every look and tone assures me that you blame me for this mishap.'

"Was he daring me? If so, he should find me his equal. I raised my eyes and surveyed him.

"'Shall I tell you why this is so—why I associate Miss Leighton's caprice with your return, and regard both with suspicion? Because I have seen you look on her with love; because I have surprised the passion in your face and beheld her—'

"'Well?'

"The tone was indescribable. It was as if a hand had taken me by the throat and choked me. I drew off and was silent.

"He seized the word at once.

"'You have seen nothing. If you think you have, then have you deceived yourself. Marah Leighton has beauty, but it is not a kind that moves me—'

"He paled. Was it horror of the lie he was uttering? I have never known, never shall know.

"'The woman I am going to marry is Honora Dudleigh.'

"I gazed at him, determined to find the truth if it were in him. He bore my look unflinchingly, though his color did not return, and his hands trembled nervously.

"'You love her?' I asked.

"'I love her,' he returned.

"'And your wedding day—'

"'Is set.'

"'May it have no interruptions,' I remarked.

"He laughed—an uneasy laugh, I thought—but jealousy was not yet dead within me.

"'And yours?' he inquired.

"'I have had mine,' I returned. 'I shall never have another.'

"He shook his head and looked at me inquisitively. I repeated my assertion.

"'I shall never approach the altar again with a woman. I am done with such things, and done with love.'

"He finished his laugh.

"'Wait till you see Marah Leighton smile again,' he cried; and with the first reappearance of his old manner that I had seen in him since the beginning of this interview, he caught up a wine glass off the table, and filling it with wine, exclaimed jovially: 'Here's to our future wives! May they be all that love paints them!'

"I thought his mirth indecent, his manner out of keeping with the occasion, and the whole situation atrocious. But I saw he was about to leave, and said nothing; but I did not drink his toast. When he was gone, I broke his glass by flinging it at my own reflection, in a glass I had bought to mirror her beauty; and before the day was spent, I had destroyed every destructible article in the house whose value or whose prettiness spoke of the attempt I had made to alter my home from a bachelor's abode to the nest I had thought in keeping with the dove I had failed to place there. As I did it I filled the house with mocking laughter; that I should have thought that this or that would please her, who would have found a palace open to criticism, and the splendors of a throne room scarce grand enough for her taste! I was but suffering the stings of a lifetime compressed into a day, and was miserable because I could see no prospect but further addition to my suffering."

CHAPTER XIII

BEFORE THE WEDDING

"Two weeks after this I was sitting beside my solitary hearth, musing upon my misery and longing for the blessed relief of sleep. There was no one with me in the house. I had dismissed every servant; for I would have no spies about me, prying into my misery; and though I could not keep the world of men and women from my doors, I could at least refuse to admit them; and this I did—living the life of a recluse almost as much as I do here, but with less ease, because the wind would bring whispers, and the walls were not thick enough to shut out from my fancy the curious glances I felt to be cast upon them by every passer-by that wandered through the street.

"On this night I had been thinking of Miss Dudleigh, of whose visibly failing health various murmurs had reached me, and I felt, notwithstanding my determination to hold myself aloof from every one and everything that could in any way reopen my still smarting wound, I could more easily find the sleep I longed for if some word from the great house would relieve the suspense in which my ignorance kept me. But I would not go there if I died of my anxiety, nor would I stoop to question any of the market men or women, who were the only persons admitted now within my doors.

"The clock was striking, and the strange sense of desolation which is inseparable from this sound to a solitary man (you see I have no clock here) was stealing over me, when I heard a tap on one of the windows overlooking my small garden, and a voice came through the lattice, crying:

"'Massa—Massa Felt.'

"I knew the voice at once. It was that of one of Miss Dudleigh's servants, an honest black, who had always been devoted to me from the day he did me some trifling service with Miss Leighton. Hearing it now, and after such thoughts, I was so moved by the promise it gave of news from the one quarter I desired, that I stumbled as I rose, and found difficulty in answering him. Nor did I recover my self-possession for hours; for the story he had to tell—after numerous apologies for his presumption in disturbing me—was so significant of coming evil that my mind was thrown again into turmoil, and the passions which I had tried to smother were roused again into action.

"It was simply this: That one evening after Mr. Urquhart's departure, and the extinguishing of all the lights in the house, he had occasion to cross the garden. That in doing this he had heard voices, and, stepping cautiously forward, perceived, lying upon the snow-covered ground, near a certain belt of evergreens, the shadows of two persons, whose forms were hidden from his sight. Being both curious and concerned, he halted before coming too close and, listening, heard Mr. Urquhart's voice, and presently that of Miss Leighton, both speaking very earnestly.

"'Will you undertake it? Can you go through with it without shrinking?' was what the former had said.

"'I will undertake it, and I can go through with it,' was what the latter had replied.

"Frightened at a discovery which might mean nothing and which might mean misery to a mistress the day of whose marriage was scarcely a month away, the negro held his breath, determined to hear more. He was immediately rewarded by catching the words: 'You are a brave girl and my queen!' and then something like a prayer for a kiss, or some such favor, as a seal to their compact. But to this she returned a vigorous 'No,' followed by the mysterious sentence: 'I shall give you nothing till I am dead, and then I will give you everything.'

"After which they made a move as if to separate, which action so alarmed the now deeply disconcerted negro that he drew back in haste, hiding behind some neighboring bushes till they had passed him and disappeared, he out of the gate, and she through the small side entrance into the house. This was the previous night, and for nearly twenty-four hours the poor negro had tortured himself as to what he should do with the information thus surreptitiously gained. He lacked the courage to tell his mistress, and finally he had thought of me, who was her best friend, and who must have known there was something amiss with Miss Leighton, or why had I not married her when everything was ready and the minister waiting with his book in his hand?

"Not answering this insinuation, I put to him one or two of the many questions that were burning in my brain. Had he told any of the other servants what he had seen? And did Miss Dudleigh look as if she suspected there was anything wrong?

"He answered that he had not dared to speak a word of it even to his wife; and as for Miss Dudleigh, she was ill so much of the time that it was hard to tell whether she had any other cause for uneasiness or not. He only knew that she was greatly changed since this miserable deceiver came into the house.

"I believed him, and amid all my struggle and wrath tried to fix my mind upon her alone. I succeeded only partially, but enough to enable me to write this line, which I entreated him to carry to her:

'HONORED MISS DUDLEIGH—You will forgive me if I overstep the bounds of friendship in yielding to the inner voice which compels me to say that if before or on your marriage day you need advice or protection, you may command both from

Your respectful servant, 'MARK FELT.'

"I did not expect a reply to this note, and I did not receive any. I thought I went as far as my position toward her allowed, but I have questioned it since—questioned if I should not have told her what the negro had heard and seen, and let her own judgment decide her fate. But I was not in my right mind in those days. I was too much a part of all this misery to be a fair judge of my own duty; and then the mysterious nature of Miss Leighton's remark, the incomprehensibility of the words—'I shall give you nothing till I am dead, and then I shall give you everything'—added such unreality to the scene, and awakened such curious conjectures, that I did not know where any of us stood, or to what especial misery the future pointed.

"'Till she was dead!' What could she, what did she mean? She would then give him everything! Ah! ah!—when she was dead! Well, so be it. Meanwhile, there was no prospect of death for any one, unless it was for Miss Dudleigh, whom rumor acknowledged to be still fading, though everything was being done for her comfort, and physician after physician employed.

"I saw Cæsar once again in these days. I met him in the street, seemingly greatly to his delight, for he smiled till his teeth shone from ear to ear, and made haste to remark, in quite a jovial voice:

"'I specs it's all right, massa. Massa Urquhart never looks at Miss Leighton now, but always doin' his best for missus, making her smile quite happy when she isn't coughing that dreadful cough. We will have a gay wedding yet. Yes; Miss Leighton seems to spect that; for she all de time making pretty things and trying them on missus, and laughing and cheering her up, just as if she didn't spect any one to die.'

"Yes, but this change of manner frightened me. I grew feverishly anxious, and spent night and day in asking myself unanswerable questions. Nor did these in any way abate when one day I was startled by the tidings that all preparations for refitting the great house had stopped; that the doctors had decided that Miss Dudleigh must remove to a warmer climate, and that accordingly upon her marriage she and her husband would set sail for the Bermudas, there to take up their abode till her health was quite restored. I doubted my ears; I doubted the facts; I doubted Urquhart, and I doubted one other most of all whose name I find it hard to mention even to myself.

"Yet I should not have doubted her; I should have remembered the flame that was always burning in the depths of her eyes, and had confidence in that, if in nothing else. What if she had always been cold to me; she was not cold to him, and I should have known this and prepared myself. But I did not. I knew neither the extent of his villainy nor that of her despair. Had I done so, I might not have been crouching here a disappointed and hopeless man, while she—

"But I am running beyond my tale. After the news I had just imparted, I heard nothing more till the very week of the wedding. Then one of Miss Dudleigh's servants came to me with a note, the result of which was, that I walked out in the afternoon, and that she passed me in her carriage, and seeing me, stopped the horses and took me in, and that we rode on a short distance together.

"'I wish to talk to you,' she said. 'I wish to proffer you a request; to beg of you a favor. I want you,' she stammered and her eyes filled with tears, 'to see me married.'

"I opened my eyes with a quick denial, but I closed them again without speaking. After all, why not please her? Could I suffer more at this wedding than in thinking over it in my dungeon of a room at home? She would be there, of course, but I need not look at her; and if he or she meditated any treachery, where ought I to be but in the one place where my presence would be most useful? I decided to gratify Miss Dudleigh, almost before the inquiry in her eyes had changed to a look of suspense. 'Yes, I will come,' said I.

"She drew a deep breath, and smiled with tender sweetness.

"'I thank you,' she rejoined. 'I thank you most deeply and most truly. I do not know why I desired it so much. Possibly because I feel something like a sister to you, possibly because I feel afraid—'

"She stopped, blushing. 'I do not mean afraid. Why should I feel afraid? Edwin is very good to me; very good. I did not know he could be so attentive.' And she sighed.

"I felt that sigh go through and through me. Looking at her I took a sudden resolution.

"'Honora,' I said (I had never called her by her first name before), 'do not give your happiness into Edwin Urquhart's keeping. You have yet three days before you for reconsideration. Break your bonds, and, unhampered by uncongenial ties, seek in another climate for that peace of mind you will never enjoy here or elsewhere as his wife.'

"She stared at me for a moment with wide-open and appealing eyes; then she shook her head, and answered quietly:

"'One broken-off wedding in the family is enough. I cannot shock society with another. But, oh, Mark! why did you not warn me at first? I think I would have listened; I think so.'

"'Forgive me,' I entreated. 'You know it would have been presumptuous in me at first; afterward she stood in the way.'

"'I know,' she answered, and turned away her head.

"I saw she did not wish me to leave her yet; so I said:

"'You are going away; you are going to leave Albany.'

"'I must, or so Edwin thinks. He says I will never recover in this climate.'

"'Do you wish to go?'

"'Yes; I think I do. I can never be happy here, and perhaps when we are far away, and have only each other to think of, the love and confidence of which I have dreamed may come. At all events, I comfort myself with that hope.'

"'But it is a long, long sea voyage. Have you strength enough to carry you through?'

"'If I have not,' she intimated, with a mournful smile, 'he will be free, and I released without scandal from a marriage that fills you with apprehension.'

"'Oh,' I cried, 'would I were your brother indeed! This should never go on.' Then impelled by what I thought to be my duty, I inquired: 'And your money, Honora?'

"She flushed, but answered in the same spirit in which I had spoken.

"'As little of it as may be will remain with him. That much my old guardian insisted upon. Do not ask me any more questions, Mark.'

"'None of a nature so personal,' I promised. 'But there is one thing—can you not guess what it is?—which I ought to know. It is about Marah.'

"The words came with effort, and hurt her as much as me. But she answered bravely:

"'She returns to Schenectady the same day that we depart. I hoped she would not linger to the wedding, but she seems to have a strange desire to face again the people who have talked about her so freely these last few weeks. So what can I say to dissuade her?'

"'Let her stay,' I muttered; 'but let her beware how she behaves on that day, for there will be two eyes watching her, prompt to see any treachery, and prompt, too, to avenge it.'

"'You will have nothing to avenge,' murmured Honora; 'that is all in the past.'

"I prayed to Heaven she might be right, and ere long bowed in adieu and left her. I saw neither herself nor any one else again till I entered the Dudleigh mansion three days later to witness her nuptials."

CHAPTER XIV

A CASSANDRA AT THE GATE

"Miss Dudleigh, moved, perhaps, by the unpleasant eclat which had followed the broken-off marriage of her cousin, chose to celebrate her own wedding in her own house, and with as little ceremony as possible. Only her most intimate friends, therefore, were invited, but these were numerous enough to fill the halls and most of the lower rooms.

"When I entered there was a sudden cessation of conversation; but this I had expected. If anything could add to the interest of the occasion, certainly it was my presence; and, feeling this, I made them all a profound obeisance, and, neither shirking their glances nor inviting them, I took my place in the spot I had chosen for myself, and waited, with a face as impassive as a mask, but with a heart burning with fury and love, not for the coming of the bride, but of her who in this hour ought to have been standing at my side as my wife.

"But I miscalculated if I thought she would enter with them. Even her bold and arrogant spirit shrank from a position so conspicuous, and it was not till they had presented themselves and taken their places in front of the latticed window so associated with my past, that I felt that peculiar sensation which always followed the entrance of Marah into the same room with myself, and, yielding to the force that constrained me, I searched the throng with eager looks, and there, where the crowd was thickest, and the shadow deepest, I saw her. She was gazing straight at me, and there was in her great eyes a look which I did not then understand, and about which I have since tortured myself by asking again and again if it were remorse, entreaty, farewell, or despair that spoke through it. Sometimes I have thought it was fear. Sometimes— But why conjecture? It was an unreadable expression to me then, and even in remembrance it is no clearer. Whatever it betokened, my pride bent before it, and a flood of the old feeling rushed over my heart, making me quite weak for a moment.

"But I conquered myself, as far as all betrayal of my feelings was concerned, and turning from the spot that so enthralled me, I fixed my gaze upon the bride.

"She was looking beautiful; more beautiful than any one had seen her look for weeks. A bright color suffused her delicate cheeks, and in her eyes burned a strange excitement, which did the work of happiness in lighting up her face. But it was a transient glow which faded imperceptibly but surely, as the ceremony proceeded, and passed completely away as the last inexorable words were uttered which made her the wife of the false being at her side.

"He, on the contrary, was pale up to that same critical moment—very pale, when one remembers his naturally florid complexion; but as her color went, his rose, and when the minister withdrew, and friends began to crowd around them, he grew so jovial and so noisy that more than one person glanced at him with suspicion, and cast pitying looks at the now quiet and immobile young wife.

"Meantime I sought with eager anxiety to catch one more glimpse of Marah. But she had shrunk from sight, and was not to be found. And the gayety ran high and the wine was poured freely, and the bridegroom drank with ever-increasing excitement, toasting his bride, but never looking at her, though her eyes turned more than once upon him with an appeal that affected painfully more than one person in the crowd. At last she rose, and, at this signal, he put down his glass, and, with a low bow to the company, prepared to follow her from the room. They passed close to the place where I stood, and I caught one glance from his eyes. It was a laughing one, but there was uneasiness in it. There might have been something more, but I had not time to search for it, for at that moment I felt her dress brush against my sleeve, and turned to give her the smile which I knew her friendly heart demanded.

"'You will wait till we go?' fell in a whisper from her lips; and I nodded with another smile, and they went on and I stood where they had left me, in one of those moods which made me, as far as all human intercourse is concerned, as much of an isolated being as I am in these mountains. I did not wake again from this abstraction till that same premonitory feeling, of which I have so often spoken, told me that something in which I was deeply interested was about to happen. Looking up, I found myself in the room alone. During the hour of my abstraction the guests had gone out, and I had neither noticed their departure nor the gradual cessation of the noise which at one time had filled my ears with hubbub. But the bride had not gone. She was at that moment coming down the stairs, and it was this fact which had pierced to my inner consciousness, and aroused once more in me a vivid sense of my surroundings. He was with her, and behind them, gliding like a wraith from landing to landing, came Marah, clad like the bride in a traveling dress, but without the bonnet which betokened an instant departure.

"Not anticipating her presence so near, I felt my courage fail, and pushing forward, joined the group of servants at the door. They, seeing in this departure of their mistress a possibly endless separation, were weeping and uttering exclamations that not only showed their devotion, but their fears. Shocked lest these words should reach her ears, I quieted them; and then seeing that the carriage which stood outside had a stranger for a driver, and that there was no accompanying wagon filled with their body servants and baggage, I asked the friendly Cæsar, who had pressed close to my side, if Mrs. Urquhart was not going to take a maid with her.

"The negro at once growled out an injured 'No!' and when I expressed my astonishment, he explained that 'There was no one here good enough to please Massa Urquhart. That he was going to pick up with some one in New York. That, though missus was sick, he would not even let her have her own gal go wid her as far as the city; said he would do everything for her hisself—as if any man could do for missus like her own Sally, who had been wid her ever since 'fore she was born!'

"'And the baggage?' I asked, troubled more than I can say by what certainly augured anything but favorably for her future.

"'Oh, massa send dat round to his house. He got books, an' a lot o' things to add to it. Dere's enough o' dat; an' den more went down de ribber on a sloop a week an' more ago.'

"'So! so! And they are going to ride?'

"'Yes, sah. You see, dey want to catch de ship w'at set sail for Bermudas, an' got to hurry; so massa says.'

"By this time Urquhart and his bride had reached the door. He was still gay and she was still quiet. But in her eye glistened a tear, while in his there gleamed nothing softer than that vague spark of triumph which one might expect to see in a man who had just married the richest heiress in Albany.

"'Good-by! good-by! good-by!' came in soft tones from her lips; and she was just stepping over the threshold, when there suddenly appeared at the foot of the steps an old crone, so seamed and bowed with age, so weird and threatening of aspect, that we all started back appalled, and were about to draw Mrs. Urquhart out of her path, when the unknown creature raised her voice, and pointing with one skinny hand straight into the bride's face, shrieked:

"'Beware of oak walls! Beware of oak walls! They are more dangerous to you than fire and water! Beware of oak walls!'

"A shriek interrupted her. It came, not from the bride, but from the interior of the well-nigh forsaken hall behind us.

"Instantly the old crone drew herself up into an attitude more threatening and more terrible than before.

"'And you,' she cried, pointing now beyond us toward a figure which I could feel shrinking in inexplicable terror against the wall. 'And you cannot trust them either! There is death within oak walls. Beware! beware!'

"A curse, a rush, and Edwin Urquhart had flung himself at the old witch's throat. But he fell to the pavement without touching her. With the utterance of her last word, she had slipped from before our eyes and melted into the crowd which curiosity and interest had drawn within the gates, to watch this young couple's departure.

"'Who was that creature? Let me have her! Give her up, I say!' leaped from the infuriated bridegroom's lips, as he rushed up and down before the crowd with threatening arms and flashing eyes.

"But there was no response from the surging throng; while from his frightened wife such an appealing cry rung out that he returned from the vain pursuit, and regaining his place at Honora's side, put her into the carriage. But as he did so he could not refrain from casting a stealthy look behind him, which betrayed to me, if to no one else, that his anger was more on account of the words uttered to Marah than to the tender being clinging to his arm. And a jealous fury took hold of me also, and I should not have been sorry if I had seen him fall then and there, the victim of a thunderbolt more certain, if not more terrible, than that which had just overwhelmed the two women nearest to our hearts.

"'Good-by! good-by! good-by!' came again from the bride's pale lips; and this time I felt that the words were for me, and I waved my hand in response, but could not speak. And so they rode away, followed by the lamentations of the servants, from whom the old crone's ominous outburst had torn the last semblance of self-control.

"'Another carriage for Miss Leighton!' I now heard uttered somewhere like a command. And startled at the pang it caused me, I darted back into the house, determined to have one parting word with my lost love.

"She was not there, nor could she be found by any searching."

CHAPTER XV

THE CATASTROPHE

"I have but little more to tell," Mark Felt continued, "but that little is everything to me.

"When we became positively assured that Miss Leighton had disappeared from the house and would not be on hand to take the stage to Schenectady, the excitement, which had been increasing on all sides since the ceremony, culminated, and the whole town was set agog to find her, if only to solve the mystery of a nature whose actions had now become inexplicable.

"I was the first to start the pursuit. Haunted by her last look, and thrilled to every extremity by the terror of the shriek she had uttered, I did not wait for the alarm to become public, but rushed immediately up stairs at the first intimation of her disappearance.

"Though I had never pierced those regions before, my good or evil fate took me at once to a room which I saw at one glance to be hers. The boxes waiting to be carried down, the tags and ends of ribbons that I recognized, the nameless something which speaks of one particular personality and no other, all were there to assure me that I stood in the chamber which for six months or more had palpitated with the breath of the one being I loved.

"But of that I dared not think; it was no time for dreams; and only stopping to see that her bonnet had been taken, but her gloves left, I hurried down again and out of the house.

"An impulse which I cannot understand took me to Edwin Urquhart's house, or, rather, to that portion of a house which he had hired for his use since he had been looking forward to his marriage with Miss Dudleigh. Why I should go there I cannot say, unless jealousy whispered that only in this place could she hope for one final word with him, as he and his bride stopped at the door for his portion of the baggage. Be this as it may, I turned neither to right nor left till I came to his house, and when I had reached it I found that, with all my haste, I was too late, for not a soul was in its empty rooms, while far down the street which leads to the bridge I saw a carriage disappearing, which, from the wagon following it so closely, I knew to be the one containing Urquhart and his bride.

"'She has not been here,' thought I, 'or I should have met her, unless—' and my eye stole with a certain shrinking terror toward the river which skirted along the garden at the back—'unless'— But even my thoughts stopped here. I would not, could not, think of what, if it were true, would end all things for me.

"Leaving this place, I wandered aimlessly through the streets, studying each face that I met for intimations which should guide me in my search. If not a madman, I was near enough to one to make the memory of that hour hideous to me; and when at last, worn out as much by my emotions as by the countless steps I had taken, I returned to my house for a bite and sup, something in the sight of its desolation overpowered me, and yielding to a despair which assured me that I should never again see her in this world, I sank on the floor inert and powerless, and continued thus till morning, without movement and almost without consciousness.

"Fatal repose! And yet I do not know if I should call it so. It only robbed me of a few hours less of conscious misery. For when I roused, when I became again myself, and looked about my house, there on the floor, underneath a curtain window which had been left unlatched, I saw a letter containing these words:

'HONORED AND MUCH ABUSED FRIEND:—When you read this, Marah will be no more. After all that has passed—after our broken marriage and the departure of my cousin—life has become insupportable; and, believing that you would rather know me dead than miserable, I ventured to write you these words, and ask you to forgive me, now that I am gone.

'I loved him: let that explain everything.
'Despairingly yours,
'MARAH LEIGHTON.'

"With shrieks I tore from the house. Marah dying! Marah dead! I would see about that. Racing down to the gate, I paused. Some one was leaning on it. It was Cæsar, and at the first glimpse I had of his face I knew I was too late—that all was over, and that the whole town knew it.

"'Oh, massa, I wanted to go in, but I was frightened. I's been waiting here an hour, sah; when dey told me dat dey had found her bonnet floating on de ribber, I know'd how you'd feel, sah, and so I come here and—'

"I found words to ask him a question. 'When was this found, and where?'

"'This morning, sah, at daybreak. It was caught by one of the strings to that old log, sah, that lies out in the ribber back of—' he hesitated—'Massa Urquhart's house, sah.'

"I knew; and I had glanced that way just as her bright head was perhaps sinking under the water. I threw up my arms in anguish and stumbled back into the house.

"'Then every one knows—' I managed to say on the threshold.

"'Dat she cared for him? Yes, sah; I fear so. How could dey help it, sah? Mor'n one person saw her run down de street and go into massa's old house just before de carriage stopped thar, and as she didn't come out again, I 'specs it was from dat big log at the foot of the garden she jumped into de ribber. All de folks pities you very much, sah—'

"I choked him off with a look.

"'Who has been sent after Mr. and Mrs. Urquhart to inform them of what has happened?'

"'No one yet, sah. But Massa Hatton—'

"'Mr. Hatton is an old man. We must have a young one for this business. Go saddle me the quickest horse in your stables. I will ride after them, and overtake them, too, before they can reach Poughkeepsie. He shall know—'

"A glance from the negro's eye warned me to be careful. I smothered my impatience and let only my earnestness appear.

"'Mrs. Urquhart ought to know that her cousin is dead,' I declared.

"'I'll tell Massa Hatton,' said the black.

"But my caution was now too much aroused for me to make Mr. Hatton the medium of my request—he was Mrs. Urquhart's old guardian and future agent; and subduing the extreme fury of my feelings, I obtained his permission to act as his messenger. Had he known of the letter which had been thrown into my window, he might not have given his consent so freely; but I had told no man of that, and he and others saw me ride away without a seeming suspicion of the murderous thoughts that struggled with my grief, and almost overwhelmed it.

"For to me her death—if she were dead—was the result of a compact entered into with the despicable Urquhart, who, if he could not have her for himself, was willing she should go where no other man could have her. Though the idea seemed quixotic, though it be an anomaly in human experience, for a woman thus to sacrifice herself, I could not ascribe any other motive to her deed; for the memory of that interview she had held with her cousin's future husband in the garden was still fresh in my mind. Do you remember the words as told me by the negro who overheard them? First, the question from his lips: 'Will you undertake it? Can you go through with it without shrinking and without fear?' And the reply from hers: 'I will undertake it, and I can go through with it,' followed by that assurance which struck me as being so inexplicable at the time, and which, with all the light that this late horrible event has thrown upon it, still preserves its mystery for me. 'I shall give you nothing till I am dead, and then I will give you everything.' If the conclusions I drew seemed wild, were they not warranted by these words? Did she not speak of death, and did he not encourage her?

"If she were not dead—and sometimes this thought would cross my burning brain—then she was with him, forced into the company of his unwilling wife in that last interview which they must have held in his cottage. In either case he was a villain and a coward, deserving of death; and death he should have, and from the hand of him whom he had doubly outraged.

"But as I rode out of town and came in sight of the river, I found myself seized by terrifying thoughts. Should I have to ride by the place where I could see them stooping with boat hooks and bending with peering eyes over some snag they had brought up from the river bottom? Could I endure to face this picture, then to pass it, then to ride on, feeling it ever at my back, blackening the morning, destroying the noontide, making more horrible the night? Could I go from this place till I knew whether or not the sullen waters would yield up their beautiful prey, and would my body proceed while my heart was on this river bank, and my jealousy divided between the wretch who had urged her on to death and these other men who might yet touch her unconscious form and gaze upon her disfigured beauty? And the answer which welled up from within me was, yes, I could go; I could pass that picture; I could feel it glooming ever and ever upon me from behind my back, and never turn my head;—such an impetus of hate was upon me, driving me forward after the wretch fleeing in self-complacency and triumph into a future of wealth and social consideration.

"But when I had done all this, when my too fleet horse had carried me beyond sight of the city, and nature, with its irresistible beauty, had begun to influence my understanding, other thoughts came trooping in upon me, and a vision of Honora Dudleigh's face as she took the dagger from my hands and an implied promise from my lips, rose before me till I could see nothing else. Honora, Honora, Honora who trusted me! who had suffered everything but the sight of blood! who was a bride, and whom it would be base ingratitude for me to plunge into the depths of dishonor and despair! And the struggle was so fierce, and the torture of it so keen, that ere long my brain succumbed to the strain, and from the height of anguished feeling I sank into apathy, and from apathy into unconsciousness, till I no longer knew where I was or possessed power to guide my horse. In this condition I was found wandering in a field and thence carried to a farm house, where I remained a prey to fever. When I returned to consciousness, three weeks had elapsed.

"As soon as I could be moved, I went back to Albany. I found the community there settled in the belief that I had joined in death the woman I so much loved, and was shown a letter which had been sent me, and which had been opened by the authorities after all hope had been given up of my return. It was from Mrs. Urquhart, and related how they had changed their plans upon reaching New York. Having found a ship on the point of sailing for France, they had determined to go there instead of to the Bermudas, and, consequently, requested me to inform Mr. Hatton of the fact, and also assure him that he would hear from them personally as soon as a letter could reach him from the other side. As she was in haste—in truth, was writing this in the post office on the way to the ship—she would only add that her health had been improved by her long journey down the river, and that when I heard from her again, she was sure she would be able to write that all her fondest hopes had been fully realized.

"And so Marah was in the river, and Urquhart on the seas. I had been robbed of everything, even vengeance, and life had nothing for me, and I was determined to leave it, not in the vulgar way of suicide, but by cloistering myself in the great forests. As no one said me nay, I at once carried out this scheme; and to show you how dead I had become to the world, I will tell you that as I turned the lock of my door and took my first step forward on the road which led to this spot, a great shout broke out in the market place:

"'The farmers of Lexington have fired upon the king's troops!'

"And I did not even turn my head!"

CHAPTER XVI

A DREAM ENDED

There was silence in the cave. Mark Felt's story was at an end.

For a moment I sat and watched him; then, as I realized all that I must yet gather from his lips, I broke the stillness by saying, in my lowest and most suggestive tone, these two words:

"And Marah?"

The name did not seem unwelcome. Striking his breast, he cried:

"She lies here! Though she despised me, deceived me, broke my heart in life, and in death betrayed a devotion for another that was at once my dishonor and the downfall of my every hope, I have never been able to cast her out of my heart. I love her, and shall ever love her, and so I am never lonely. For in my dreams I imagine that death has changed her. That she can see now where truth and beauty lie; that she would fain come back to them and me; and that she does, walking with softened steps through the forest, beaming upon me in the moon rays and smiling upon me in the sunshine till—"

Great sobs broke from the man's surcharged breast. He flung himself down on the floor of the cave and hid his face in his hands. He had forgotten that I had come on an errand of vengeance. He had forgotten the object of that vengeance; he had forgotten everything but her.

I saw the mistake I had made, and for the moment I quailed before the prospect of rectifying it. He had shown me his heart. I had peered into its depths, and it seemed an impossible thing to tear the last hope from his broken life; to show her in her true light to his horrified eyes; to tell him she was not dead; that it was Honora Urquhart who was dead; and that the woman he mourned and beheld in his visions as a sanctified spirit was not only living upon the fruits of a crime, but triumphing in them; that, in short, he had thrown away communion with men to brood upon a demon.

My feelings were so strong, my shrinking so manifest, that he noticed them at last. Rising up, he surveyed me with a growing apprehension.

"How you look at me!" he cried. "It is not only pity for the past I see in your eyes, but fear for the future. What is it? What can threaten me now of importance enough to call up such an expression to your face? Since Marah is dead—"

"Wait!" I cried. "First let me ask if Marah is dead." His face, which was turned toward me, grew so pale I felt my own heart contract.

"If—Marah—is—dead!" he gasped, growing huskier with each intonation till the last word was almost unintelligible.

"Yes," I continued, ignoring his glance and talking very rapidly; "her body was never found. You have no proof that she perished. The letter that she wrote you may have been a blind. Such things have happened. Try and remember that such things have happened."

He did not seem to hear me. Turning away, he looked about him with wide-open and questioning eyes, like a child lost in a wood.

"I cannot follow you," he murmured. "Marah living?" His own words seemed to give him life. He turned upon me again. "Do you know that she is living?" he asked. "Is it this you have come to tell me? If so, speak, speak! I can bear the news. I have not lost all firmness. I—I—"

He stopped and looked at me piteously. I saw I must speak, and summoned up my courage.

"Marah may not be living," I said, "but she did not perish in the river. It would have been better for you, though, and infinitely better for her if she had. She only lived to do evil, Mr. Felt. In bemoaning her you have wasted a noble manhood."

"Oh!"

The cry came suddenly, and rang through the cavern like a knell. I could not bear it, and hurried forward my revelation.

"You tell me that you received a letter from Mrs. Urquhart before she set sail for France. Was it the only letter which she has ever sent you? Have you never heard from her since?"

"Never!" He looked at me almost in anger. "I did not want to. I bade the postmaster to destroy any letters which came for me. I had cut myself loose from the world."

"Have you that letter? Did you keep it?"

"No; I gave it back to the men who opened it. What was it to me?"

"Mark Felt," I now asked, "did you know Honora Dudleigh's writing?"

"Of course. Why should you question it? Why—"

"And was this letter in her writing? written by her hand?"

"Of course—of course; wasn't it signed with her name?"

"But the handwriting? Couldn't it have been an imitation? Wasn't it one? Was it not written by Marah, and not Honora? She was a clever woman, and—"

"Written by Marah? By Marah? Great heavens, did she go with them, then? Were my secret doubts right? Is she lost to me in eternity as well as here? Is she living with him?"

"She was living with him, and there is good reason to believe she is doing so still. There is a Mr. Urquhart in Paris, and a Mrs. Urquhart. As Marah is the woman he loved, she must be this latter."

"Must be? I do not see why you should say must be! Is Honora dead? Is—"

"Honora is dead—has been dead for sixteen years. The woman who sailed with Mr. Urquhart called herself Honora, but she was not Honora. She who rightfully bore this name was dead and hidden away. It is of crime that I am speaking. Edwin Urquhart is a murderer, and his victim was—"

It was not necessary to say more. In the suddenly outstretched hand, with its open palm; in the white face so drawn that his mother would not have known it; in the gradual sinking and collapsing of the whole body, I saw that I had driven the truth home at last, and that silence now was the only mercy left to show him.

I was silent, therefore, and waited as we wait beside a death bed for the final sigh of a departing spirit. But life, and not death, was in the soul of this man before me. Ere long he faintly stirred, then a smothered moan left his lips, followed by one word, and that word was the echo of my own:

"Murder."

The sound it made seemed to awake whatever energy of horror lay dormant within him. Bestirring himself, he lifted his head and repeated again that fearsome word:

"Murder!"

Then he leaped to his feet, and his aspect grew terrible as he looked up and shouted, as it were, into the heavens that same dread word:

"Murder!"

Filled with horror, I endeavored to take him by the arm, but he shook me off, and cried in a terrible voice:

"A fiend, a demon, a creature of the darkest hell! I have worshiped her, pardoned her, dreamed of her for fifteen years in solitudes dedicated to God! O Creator of all good! What sacrilege I have committed! How shall I ever atone for a manhood wasted on a dream, and for thoughts that must have made the angels of Heaven veil their faces in wonder and pity.

"You must have a story to tell," he now said, turning toward me, with the first look of natural human curiosity which I had seen in his face since I came.

"Yes," said I, "I have; but it will not serve to lessen your horror; it will only add to it."

"Nothing can add to it," was his low reply. "And yet I thank you for the warning."

Encouraged by his manner, which had become strangely self-possessed, I immediately began, and told him of the visit of this bridal party at your inn; then as I saw that he had judged himself correctly, and that he was duly prepared for all I could reveal, I added first your suspicions, and then a full account of our fatal discovery in the secret chamber.

He bore it like a man upon whom emotion has spent all its force; only, when I had finished, he gave one groan, and then, as if he feared I would mistake the meaning of this evidence of suffering, he made haste to exclaim:

"Poor Honora! My heart owes her one cry of pity, one tear of grief. I shall never weep for any one else; though, if I could, it would be for myself and the wasted years with which I have mocked God's providence."

Relieved to find him in this mood, I rose and shook his hand cordially.

"You will come back to Albany with me?" I entreated. "We have need of you, and this spot will never be a home to you again."

"Never!"

The echo was unexpected, but welcome. I led the way out of the cave.

"See! it is late," I urged.

He shook his head and cast one prolonged look around him.

"What do I not leave behind me here? Love, grief, dreams. And to what do I go forward? Can you tell me? Has the future in it anything for a man like me?"

"It has vengeance!"

He gave a short cry.

"In which she is involved. Talk to me not of that! And yet," he presently added, "what it is my duty to do, I shall do. It is all that is left to me now. But I will do nothing for vengeance. That would be to make a slave of myself again."

I had no answer for this, and therefore gave none. Instead I shouted to my guide, and after receiving from him such refreshments as my weary condition demanded, I gave notice that I was ready to descend, and asked the recluse if he was ready to accompany me.

He signified an instant acquiescence, and before the sun had quite finished its course in the west we found ourselves at the foot of the mountains. As civilization broke upon us Mr. Felt drew himself up, and began to question me about the changes which the revolution had made in our noble country.

I will not weary you, my dear Mrs. Truax, with the formalities which followed upon our return to Albany. I will merely add that you may expect a duly authorized person to come to you presently for such testimony in this matter as it may be in your power to give; after which a suitable person will proceed to France with such papers as may lead to the delivering up of these guilty persons to the United States authorities; in which case justice must follow, and your inn will be avenged for the most hideous crime which has ever been perpetrated within our borders.

Most respectfully,
ANTHONY TAMWORTH.

PART III

RETRIBUTION

CHAPTER XVII

STRANGE GUESTS

SEPTEMBER 29, 1791.

Two excitements to-day. First, the appearance at my doors of the person of whose coming I was advised by Mr. Tamworth. He came in his own carriage, and is a meager, hatchet-faced man, whose eye makes me restless, but has not succeeded in making me lose my self-possession. He stayed three hours, all of which he made me spend with him in the oak parlor, and when he had finished with me and got my signature to a long and complicated affidavit, I felt that I would rather sell my house and flee the place than go through such another experience. Happily it is likely to be a long time before I shall be called upon to do so. A voyage to France and back is no light matter; and what with complications and delays, a year or more is likely to elapse before the subject need be opened again in my hearing. I thank God for this. For not only shall I thus have the opportunity of regaining my equanimity, which has been sorely shaken by these late events, but I shall have the chance of adding a few more dollars to my store, against the time when scandal will be busy with this spot, and public reprobation ruin its excellent character and custom.

The oak parlor I have shut and locked. It will not be soon entered again by me.

The other excitement to which I referred was the coming of two new guests from New York, elegant ladies, whose appearance and manners quite overpowered me in the few minutes of conversation I held with them when they first entered my house.

Good God! what is that? I thought I felt something brush my sleeve. Yet there is no one near me, and nothing astir in the room! And why should such a sudden vision of the old oak parlor rise before my eyes? And why, if I must see it, should it be the room as it looked to me on that night when the two Urquharts sat within it, and not the room as I saw it to-day!

Positively I must throw away the key of that room; its very presence in my desk makes me the victim of visions.

OCTOBER 5, 1791.

Why is it that we promise ourselves certain things, even swear that we will perform such and such acts, and yet never keep our promises or hold to our oaths? Sixteen years ago I expressed a determination to refit the oak parlor and make it look more attractive to the eye; I never did it. A year since I declared in language as strong as I knew how to employ, not that I would refit the oak parlor, but that I would tear it from the house, even at the cost of demolishing the whole structure.

And now, only a week since, I promised myself, as my diary will testify, that I would throw away the key of this place, if only to rid myself of unpleasant reminders. But the key is still with me, and the room intact. I have neither the power nor the inclination to touch it. The ghost of the woman who perished there restrains me. Why? Because we are not done with that room. The end of its story is not yet. This I feel; and I feel something further; I feel that it will be entered soon, and that the person who is to enter it is already in my house.

I have spoken of two ladies—God knows with but little realization of the fatal interest they would soon possess for me. They came without servants some four days ago, and saying they wished to remain for a short time in this beautiful spot, at once accepted the cheerful south room which I reserve for such guests as these. As they are very handsome and distinguished-looking, I felt highly gratified at their patronage, and was settling down to a state of complacency over the prospects of a profitable week, when something, I cannot tell what, roused in me a spirit of suspicion, and I began to notice that the elder lady was of a very uneasy disposition, exhibiting a proneness to wander about the house and glide through its passages, especially those on the ground floor, which at first made me question her sanity, and then led me to wonder if through some means unknown to me she had not received a hint as to our secret chamber. I watch, but cannot yet make out. Meanwhile a description of these women may not come amiss.

They are both beautiful, the younger especially. When I first saw them seated in my humble parlor, I thought them the wife and daughter of one of our great generals, they looked so handsome and carried themselves so proudly. But I was presently undeceived, for the name they gave was a foreign one, which my English tongue finds it very hard even yet to pronounce. It is written Letellier, with a simple Madame before it for the mother, and Mademoiselle for the daughter, but how to speak it—well, that is a small matter. I do speak it and they never smile, though the daughter's eye lights up at times with a spark of what I should call mirth, if her lips were not so grave and her brow so troubled.

Yes; troubled is the word, though she is so young. I find it difficult to regard her in any other light than that of a child. Though she endeavors to appear indifferent and has a way of carrying herself that is almost noble, there is certainly grief in her eye and care on her brow. I see it when she is alone, or rather before she becomes aware of another's presence; I see it when she is with her mother; but when strangers come in or she assembles with the rest of the household in the parlor or at the table, then it vanishes, and a sweet charm comes that reminds me—

But this is folly, sheer folly. How could she look like Mrs. Urquhart? Imagination carries me too far. Equal innocence and a like gentle temper have produced a like result in sweetening the expression. That is all, and yet I remember the one woman when I look at the other, and shudder; for the woman who calls this child daughter has her eye on the oak parlor, and may meditate evil—must, if she knows its secret and yet wishes to enter it. But my imagination is carrying me too far again. This woman, whatever her faults, loves her daughter, and where love is there cannot be danger. Yet I shudder.

Madame Letellier merits the description of an abler pen than mine. I like her, and I hate her. I admire her, and I fear her. I obey her, and yet hold myself in readiness for rebellion, if only to prove to myself that I will be strong when the time comes; that no influence, however exerted, or however hidden under winning smiles or quietly controlling glances, shall have power to move me from what I may consider my duty, or from the exercise of such vigilance as my secret fears seem to demand. I hate her; let me remember that. And I distrust her. She is here for evil, and her eye is on the oak parlor. Though it is locked and the key hidden on my person, she will find means to possess herself of that key and open that door. How? We will see. Meantime all this is not a description of Madame Letellier.

She is finely formed; she is graceful; she is youthful. She dresses with a taste that must always make her conspicuous wherever she may be. You could not enter a room in which she was without seeing her, for her glance has a strange power that irresistibly draws your glance to it, though her eyes are lambent rather than brilliant, and if large, rarely opened to their full extent. Her complexion is dark; that is, in comparison with her daughter's, which is of a marble-like purity. But it has strange flushes in it, and at times seems almost to sparkle. Her hair is brown, and worn high, with a great comb in it, setting off the contour of her face, which is almost perfect. But it is in the expression of her mouth that her fascination lies. Without sweetness, except when it smiles upon her daughter, without mirth, without any expression speaking of good-will or tenderness, there is yet a turn to the lips that moves the gazer peculiarly, making it dangerous to watch her long unless you are hardened by doubts, as I am. Her hands are exquisite, and her form beauty itself.

The daughter is statuesque; not in the sense of coldness or immobility, but in the regularity of her features and the absence of any coloring in her cheeks. She is lovely, and there breathes through every trait a gentle soul that robs my admiration of all awe and makes my old and empty heart long to serve her. Her eyes are gray and her hair a reddish brown, with kinks and curls in it like— But, pshaw! there comes that dream again! Was Honora Urquhart's hair so very unique that a head of wavy brown hair should bring her up so startlingly to my mind?

They are stopping here on their way to Albany—so the elder lady says. They came from New York. So they did, but if my intuitions are not greatly at fault, the place they started from was France. The fact that the marks and labels have all been effaced from their baggage is suspicious in itself. Can they be friends of the two miserable wretches who dishonored my house with a ghastly crime? Is it from them that madame's knowledge comes, if she has any knowledge? The thought awakens my profoundest distrust. Would that Mr. Tamworth were within reach! I think I will write him. But what could I write that would not look foolish on paper? I had better wait a while till I see something or hear something more definite.

CHAPTER XVIII

MRS. TRUAX TALKS

OCTOBER 7, 1791.

This morning I was exceedingly startled by one of my guests suddenly asking me before several of the others, if my inn had a ghost.

"A ghost!" I cried, for the moment quite aghast.

"Yes," was the reply; "it has the look of a house which could boast of such a luxury. Don't you think so, Mr. Westgate?"

This is a newcomer who had just been introduced.

"Well," observed the latter, "as I have seen only this room, and as this room is anything but ghostlike at the present moment, I hardly consider myself competent to judge."

"But the exterior! Surely you noticed the exterior. Such a rambling old structure; such a beetling top to it, as if it had settled down here to brood over a mysterious past. I never see it, especially at twilight, that I don't wonder what lies so heavily upon its conscience. Is it a crime? There would be nothing strange about it if it was. Such old houses rarely have a clean past."

It was nonchalantly said, but it sank deep into my heart. Not that I felt that he had any motive in saying it—I knew the young scapegrace too well—but that I was conscious from his first word of two eyes burning on my face, which robbed me of all self-possession, though I think I sat without movement, and only paled the slightest in the world.

"A house that dates back to a time when the white men and the red fought every inch of the territory on which it stands would be an anomaly if it did not have some drops of blood upon it," I ventured to say, as soon as I could command my emotions.

"True," broke in a low, slow voice—that of Madame Letellier. "Do you know of any especial tragedy that makes the house memorable?"

I turned and gave her a look before replying. She was seated in the shadows of a remote corner, and had so withdrawn herself behind her daughter that I could see nothing of her face. But her hands were visible, and from the force with which she held them clasped in her lap I perceived that the subject we were discussing possessed a greater interest for her than for any one else in the room. "She has heard something of the tragedy connected with this house," was my inward comment, as I prepared to answer her.

"There is one," I began, and paused. Something of the instinct of the cat with the mouse had entered into me. I felt like playing with her suspense, cruel as it may seem.

"Oh, tell us!" broke in the daughter, a sudden flush of interest suffusing for a moment her white cheek. "That is, if it is not too horrible. I never like horrible stories; they frighten me. And as for a ghost—if I thought you kept such a creature about your house, I should leave it at once."

"We have no ghosts," I answered, with a gravity that struck even myself unpleasantly, it was in such contrast to her mellow and playful tones. "Ghosts are commonplace. We countenance nothing commonplace here."

"Good!" broke in a voice from the crowd of young men. "The house is above such follies. It must have some wonderful secret, then. What is it, Mrs. Truax? Do you own a banshee? Have you a—"

"Mamma, you hurt me!"

The cry was involuntary. Madame had caught her daughter by the hand and was probably unaware what passion she had put into her clasp. Mademoiselle Letellier blushed again at the sound of her own voice, and prayed her mother's pardon with the most engaging of smiles. As she did so, I caught a glimpse of that mother's face. It was white as death. "Decidedly, she knows more than she ought to," thought I. "And yet she wants to know more. Why?"

"The Happy-Go-Lucky Inn," I observed, as soon as the flutter caused by this incident had subsided, "is no more haunted by a banshee than by a ghost. But that is not saying it should not be. It is old enough, it is respectable enough; it has traditions enough. I could tell you tales of its owners, and incidents connected with the coming and going of the innumerable guests who have frequented it both before and during the revolution, that would keep you here till morning. But the one story I will tell must suffice. We should lose our character of mystery if I told you all. Besides, how could I tell all? Who could ever tell the complete story of such a house as this?"

"Hear! hear!" cried another young man.

"Years ago—" I stopped again, wickedly stopped. "Madame, will you not come forward where it is lighter?"

"I thank you," Madame Letellier responded.

She rose deliberately and came forward, tall, mute and commanding. She sat down in the light; she looked me in the face; she robbed me even of my doubts. I felt my heart turn over in my breast and wondered.

"You do not proceed," she murmured.

"Pardon me," said I; and assuming a nonchalance I was far from feeling, I commenced again. I had played with her fears. I would play with them further. I would see how much she could bear. I resumed:

"Years ago, when I was younger and had been mistress of this place but a short time, there entered this place one evening, at nightfall, a young couple. Did you speak, madame? Excuse me, it was your daughter, then?"

"Yes," chimed in the latter, coming forward and taking her stand by the mother, greatly to the delight of the young gentlemen present, who asked for nothing better than an opportunity to gaze upon her modest but exquisite face. "Yes; it was I. I am interested, that is all."

I began to hate my role, but went on stolidly.

"They were a handsome pair, and I felt an interest in them at once. But this interest immeasurably heightened when the young man, almost before the door had closed upon them, drew me apart and said: 'Madame, we are an unhappy couple. We have been married just four hours.'"

Here I paused for breath, and to take a good look at madame.

She was fixed as a stone, but her eyes were burning. Evidently she expected the relation of a story which she knew. I would disappoint her. I would cause in her first a shock of relief, and then I would reawaken her fears and probe her very soul. Slowly, and as if it were a matter of course, I proceeded to say:

"It was a run-away match, and as the young husband remarked, 'a great disappointment to my wife's father, who is an English general and a great man. My wife loves me, and will never allow herself to be torn from me; but she is not of age, and her father is but a few minutes' ride behind us. Will you let us come in? We dare not risk the encounter on the road; he would shoot me down like a dog, and that would kill my young wife. If we see him here, he may take pity on our love, and—'

"He needed to say no more. My own compassion had been excited, as much by her countenance as by his words, and I threw open the doors of this very room.

"'Go in,' said I, 'I have a woman's heart, and cannot bear to see young people in distress. When the general comes—'

"'We shall hear him,' cried the girl; 'he has half a dozen horsemen with him. We saw them when we were on the brow of the hill.'

"'Take comfort, then,' I cried, as I closed the door, and went to see after the solitary horse which had brought them to this place.

"But before I could provide the meal with which I meant to strengthen them for the scene that must presently ensue, I heard the anticipated clattering of hoofs, and simultaneously with it, the unclosing of this door and the cry of the young wife to her husband:

"'I cannot bear it. At his first words I should fall in a faint; and how could I resist him then? No; let me fly; let me hide myself; and when he comes in, swear that you are here alone; that you brought no bride; that she left you at the altar—anything to baffle his rage and give us time.' And the young thing sprang out before me, and lifting her hands, prayed with great wide-open eyes that I would assist the lie, and swear to her father, when he came in, that her husband had ridden up alone.

"I was not as old then as I am now, I say, and I was very tender toward youthful lovers. Though I thought the scheme a wild one and totally impracticable, she so governed me by her looks and tones that I promised to do what she asked, saying, however, that if she hid herself she must do it well, for if she were found my reputation for reliability would be ruined. And standing there where you see that jog in the wall, she promised, and giving just one look of love to her companion, who stood white but firm on the threshold, she sped from our sight down the hall.

"A moment later the general's foot was where hers had been, and the general's voice was filling the house, asking for his daughter.

"'She is not here,' came from the young man in firm and stern accents. 'You have been pleased to think she was with me all these miles, but you will not find her. You can search if you please. I have nothing to say against that. But it will be time wasted.'

"'We will see about that. The girl is here, is she not?' the father asked, turning to me.

"'No,' was my firm reply; 'she is not.'

"I do not know how I managed the lie, but I did. Something in the young man's aspect had nerved me. I began to think she would not be found, though I could see no good reason for this conclusion.

"'Scatter!' he now shouted to his followers. 'Search the house well. Do not leave a nook or cranny unpenetrated. I am not General B— for nothing.' And turning to me, he added: 'You have brought this on yourself by a lie. I saw my daughter in this fellow's arms as they passed over the ridge of the hill. She is here, and in half an hour will be in my hands.'

"But the clock on the staircase struck not only the half hour, but the hour, and yet, though every room and corridor, the cellar and the garret, were searched, no token was found of the young wife's presence. Meanwhile the husband stood like a statue on the threshold, waiting with what seemed to me a strange certitude for the return of the father from his fruitless search.

"'Has she escaped from one of the windows?' I asked, moved myself to a strange curiosity.

"He looked at me, but made no reply.

"'It is dark; it is late. If the general chooses to remain here to-night—'

"'He will not find her,' was the reply.

"I was frightened—I know not why, but I was frightened. The young man had a supernatural air. I began to think of demon lovers, and was glad when the general finally appeared, storming and raving.

"'It is a conspiracy!' was his cry. 'You are all in league to deceive me. Where is my daughter, Mrs. Truax? I ask you because you have a character to lose.'

"'It is impossible for me to tell you,' was my reply. 'If she was to be found in my house, you must have found her. As you have not, there is but one conclusion to draw. She is not within these walls.'

"'She is not outside of them. I set a watch in the beginning, at the four corners of the house. None of my men have seen so much as a flutter of her dress. She is here, I say, and I ask you to give her up.'

"'This I am perfectly willing to do,' I rejoined, 'but I do not know where to find her. Let that but once be done, and I shall not stand in the way of your rights.'

"'Very well,' he cried. 'I will not search further to-night; but to-morrow—' A meaning gesture finished his sentence; he turned to the young man. 'As for you,' he cried, 'you will remain here. Unpleasant as it may be for us both, we will keep each other's company till morning. I do not insist upon conversation.' And without waiting for a reply, the sturdy old soldier took up his station in the doorway, by which action he not only shut the young man in, but gave himself a position of vantage from which he could survey the main hall and the most prominent passages.

"The rest were under charge of his followers, whom he had stationed all through the house, just as if it were in a state of siege. One guarded the east door and another the west, and on each landing of the staircase a sentinel stood, silent but alert, like a pair of living statues.

"I did not sleep that night; the mystery of the whole affair would have kept me awake even if my indignation had let me rest. I sat in the kitchen with my girls, and when the morning came, I joined the general again with offers of a breakfast.

"But he would eat nothing till he had gone through the house again; nor would he, in fact, eat here at all; for his second search ended as vainly as his first, and he was by this time so wroth, not only at the failure to recover his child, but at the loss which his dignity had suffered by this failure, that he had no sooner reached this spot, and found the young husband still standing where he had left him, than with a smothered execration, leveled not only at him, but the whole house, he strode out through the doorway, and finding his horse ready saddled in front, mounted and rode away, followed by all his troop.

"And now comes the strangest part of the tale.

"He was no sooner gone, and the dust from his horse's hoofs lost in the distance, than I turned to the young husband, and cried:

"'And now where is she? Let us have her here at once. She must be hungry, and she must be cold. Bring her, my good sir.'

"'I do not know where she is. We must be patient. She will return herself as soon as she thinks it safe.'

"I could not believe my ears.

"'You do not know where she is?' I repeated. 'How could you be so self-possessed through all these hours and all this maddened searching if you did not know she was safe?'

"'I did know she was safe. She swore to me before she set foot on your doorstep that she could so hide herself in these walls that no one could ever find her till she chose to reveal herself; and I believed her, and felt secure.'

"I did not know what to say.

"'But she is a stranger,' I murmured. 'What does she know about my house?'

"'She is a stranger to you,' he retorted, 'but she may not be a stranger to the house. How long have you lived here?'

"I could not say long. It was at the most but a year; so I merely shook my head, but I felt strangely nonplussed.

"This feeling, however, soon gave way to one much more serious as the moments fled by and presently the hours, and she did not come. We tried to curb our impatience, tried to believe that her delay was only owing to extra caution; but as morning waxed to noon, alarm took the place of satisfaction in our breasts, and we began to search the house ourselves, calling her name up and down the halls and through the empty rooms, till it seemed as if the very walls must open and reveal us the being so frantically desired.

"'She is not in the house,' I now asserted to the almost frenzied bridegroom. 'Our lies have come back upon our heads, and it is in the river we must look for her.'

"But he would not agree with me in this, and repeated again and again: 'She said she would hide here. She would not deceive me, nor would she have sought death alone. Leave me to look for her another hour. I must, I can, I will find her yet!'

"But he never did. After that last fond look with which she turned down that very hall you see before you, we saw her no more; and if my house owns no ghost and never echoes to the sound of a banshee's warning, it is not because it does not own a mystery which is certainly thrilling enough to give us either."

"Oh!" cried out several voices, as I ceased, "is that all? And what became of the poor bridegroom? And did the father ever come back? And haven't you ever really found out where the poor thing went to? And do you think she died?"

For reply I rose. I had never taken my eye off madame, and the strain upon us both had been terrible; but I let my glance wander now, and smiling genially into the eager faces which had crowded around me, I remarked:

"I never spoil a good story by too many explanations. You have heard all you will from me to-night. So do not question me further. Am I not right, madame?"

"Perfectly," came in her even tones. "And I am sure we are all very much obliged to you."

I bowed and slipped away into the background. I was worn out.

An hour later I was passing through the hall above on my way to my own room. As I passed madame's door, I saw it open, and before I had taken three steps away I felt her soft hand on my arm.

"Your pardon, Mrs. Truax," were her words; "but my daughter has been peculiarly affected by the story you related to us below. She says it is worse than any ghost story, and that she cannot rid herself of the picture of the young wife flitting out of sight down the hall. I am really afraid it has produced a very bad effect upon her, and that she will not sleep. Is it—was it a true story, Mrs. Truax, or were you merely weaving fancies out of a too fertile brain?"

I smiled, for she was smiling, and shook my head, looking directly into her eyes.

"Your daughter need not lose her sleep," I said, "on account of any story of mine. I saw they wanted something blood-curdling, so I made up a tale to please them. It was all imagination, madame; all imagination. I should not have told it if it had been otherwise. I think too much of my house."

"And you had nothing to found it upon? Just drew upon your fancy?"

I smiled. Her light tone did not deceive me as to the anxiety underlying all this; but it was not in my plan to betray my powers of penetration. I preferred that she should think me her dupe.

"Oh," I returned, as ingenuously as if I had never had a suspicious thought, "I do not find it difficult to weave a tale. Of course such a story could not be true. Why, I should be afraid to stay in the inn myself if it were. I could never abide anything mysterious. Everything with me must be as open as the day."

"And with me," she laughed; but there was a false note in her mirth, though I did not appear to notice it. "I did not suppose the story was real, but I thought you must have some old tradition to found it upon; some old wife's tale or some secret history which is a part and parcel of the house, and came to you with it."

But I shook my head, still smiling, and answered, quite at my ease:

"No old wife's tale that I have ever heard amounts to much. I can make up a better story any day than those which come down with a house like this. It was all the work of my imagination, I assure you. I tried to please them, and I hope I did it."

Her face changed at once. It was as if a black veil had been drawn away from it.

"My daughter will be so relieved," she affirmed. "I don't mind such lugubrious tales myself, but she is young and sensitive, and so tender-hearted. I am sure I thank you, Mrs. Truax, for your consideration, and beg leave to wish you a good-night."

I returned her civility, and we passed into our several rooms. Would I could know with what thoughts, for my own were as much a mystery to me as were hers.

OCTOBER 9, 1791.

Madame never addresses her daughter by her first name. Consequently we do not know it. This is a matter of surprise to the whole house, and many are the conjectures uttered by the young men as to what it can be. I have no especial curiosity about it—I would much rather know the mother's, and yet I frequently wonder; for it seems unnatural for a mother always to address her child as mademoiselle. Is she her mother? I sometimes think she is not. If the interest in the oak parlor is what I think it is, then she cannot be, for what mother would wish to bring peril to her child? And peril lies at the bottom of all interest there; peril to the helpless, the trusting and the ignorant. But is she as interested there as I thought her? I have observed nothing lately to assure me of it. Perhaps, after all, I have been mistaken.

CHAPTER XIX

IN THE HALLS AT MIDNIGHT

OCTOBER 10, 1791.

I was not mistaken. Madame is not only interested in, but has serious designs upon the oak parlor. Not content with roaming up and down the hallway leading to it, she was detected yesterday morning trying to open its door, and when politely questioned as to whom she was seeking, answered that she was looking for the sitting room, which, by the way, is on the other side of the house. And this is not all. As I lay in my bed last night resting as only a weary woman can rest, I heard a light tap at my door. Rising, I opened it, and was astonished to see standing before me the light figure of mademoiselle.

"Excuse me for troubling you," said she, in her pure English—they both speak good English, though with a foreign accent—"I am sorry to wake you, but I am so anxious about my mother. She went to bed with me, and we fell asleep; but when I woke a little while ago she was missing, and though I have waited for her a long time, she does not return. I am not well, and easily frightened! Oh, how cold it is."

I drew her in, wrapped a shawl about her, and led her back to her room.

"Your mother will return speedily," I promised. "Doubtless she felt restless, and is taking a turn or two up and down the hall."

"Perhaps; for her dressing gown and slippers are gone. But she never did anything like this before, and in a strange house—"

A slight trembling stopped the young lady from continuing.

Urging her to get into bed, I spoke one or two further words of a comforting nature, at which the lovely girl seemed to forget her pride, for she threw her arms about my neck with a low sigh, and then, pushing me softly from her, observed:

"You are a kind woman; you make me feel happier whenever you speak to me."

Touched, I made some loving reply, and withdrew. I longed to linger, longed to tell her how truly I was her friend; but I feared the mother's return—feared to miss the knowledge of madame's whereabouts, which my secret suspicion made important; so I subdued my feelings and hastened quickly to my room, where I wrapped myself in a long, dark cloak. Thus equipped, I stole back again to the hall, and gliding with as noiseless a step as possible, found my way to the back stairs, down which I crept, holding my breath, and listening intently.

To many who read these words the situation of those back stairs is well known; but there may be others who will not understand that they lead directly, after a couple of turns, to that hall upon which opens the oak parlor. Five steps from the lower floor there is a landing, and upon this landing there is a tall Dutch clock, so placed as to offer a very good hiding place behind it to any one anxious to gaze unobserved down the hall. But to reach the clock one has to pass a window, and as this looks south, and was upon this night open to the moonlight, I felt that the situation demanded circumspection.

I, therefore, paused when I reached the last step above the platform, and listened intently before proceeding further. There was no noise; all was quiet, as a respectable house should be at two o'clock in the morning. Yet from the hall below came an undefinable something which made me feel that she was there; a breathing influence that woke every nervous sensibility within me, and made my heart-beats so irregular that I tried to stop them lest my own presence should be betrayed. She was there, a creeping, baleful figure, blotting the moonshine with her tall shadow, as she passed, panther-like, to and fro before that closed door, or crouched against the wall in the same attitude of listening which I myself assumed. Or so I pictured her as I clung to the balustrade above, asking myself how I could cross that strip of moonlight separating me from that vantage-point I longed to gain. For that I knew her to be there was not enough. I must see her, and learn, if possible, what the attraction was which drew her to this fatal door. But how, how, how? If she were watching, as secrecy ever watches, I could not take a step upon that platform without being discerned. Not even if a friendly cloud came to obscure the brightness of the moon, could I hope to project my dark figure into that belt of light without discovery. I must see what was to be seen from the step where I stood, and to do this I knew but one way. Taking up the end of my long cloak, I advanced it the merest trifle beyond the edge of the partition that separated me from the hall below. Then I listened again. No sound, no stir. I breathed deeply and thrust my arm still further, the long cloak hanging from it dark and impenetrable to the floor below. Then I waited. The moonlight was not quite as bright as it had been; surely that was a cloud I saw careering over the face of the sky above me, and in another moment, if I could wait for it, the hall would be almost dark. I let my arm advance an inch or so further, and satisfied now that I had got the slit which answers for an arm-hole into a position that would afford me full opportunity of looking through the black wall I had thus improvised, I watched the cloud for the moment of comparative darkness which I so confidently expected. It came, and with it a sound—the first I had heard. It was from far down the hall, and was, as near as I could judge, of a jingling nature, which for an instant I found it hard to understand. Then the quick suspicion came as to what it was, and unable to restrain myself longer I separated the slit I have spoken of with the fingers of my right hand, and looked through.

There she was, standing before the door of the oak parlor, fitting keys. I knew it at my first glimpse, both from her attitude and the slight noise which the keys made. Taken aback, for I had not expected this, I sank out of sight, cloak and all, asking myself what I should do. I finally decided to do nothing. I would listen, and if the least intimation came to prove that she had succeeded in her endeavor, I would then spring down the steps that separated us and hold her back by the hair of her head. Meanwhile I congratulated myself that the lock of that room was a peculiar one, and that the only key I knew of that would unlock it was under the pillow of the bed I had just left.

She worked several minutes; then the moon came out. Instantly all was still. I knew whither she had gone. Near the door she was tampering with is a short passageway leading to another window. Into this she had slipped, and I could look out now with impunity, sure that she would not see me.

But I remained immovable. There was another cloud rushing up from the south, and in another moment I was confident that I should hear again the slight clatter of the key against the lock. And I did, and not only once, but several times, which fact assured me that she had not only brought a handful of keys with her, but that these keys must have come from some more distant quarter than the town; that indeed she had come provided to the Happy-Go-Lucky for this nocturnal visit, and that any doubts I might cherish were likely to have a better foundation in fact than is usual with women circumstanced like myself.

She did not succeed in her efforts. Had she brought burglar's tools I hardly think she would have been able to open that lock; as it was, there was no hope for her, and presently she seemed to comprehend this, for the slight sounds ceased and, presently, I heard a step, and peering recklessly from my corner, I perceived her gliding away toward the front stairs. I smiled, but it could not have been in a way she would have enjoyed seeing, and crept noiselessly to my own room, and our doors closed simultaneously.

This morning I watched with some anxiety for her first look. It was slightly inquiring. Summoning up my best smile, I gave her a cheerful good-morning, and then observed:

"I am glad to see you look so well this morning! Your daughter seemed to be concerned about you in the night because you had left your bed. But I told her I was sure all was right, that you were feeling nervous, and only wanted a breath of the fresh air you would find in the halls." And my glance did not flinch, nor my mouth lose its smile, though she surveyed me keenly with eyes whose look might penetrate a stone.

"You understand your own sex," was her light reply, after this short study of my face. "Yes; I was very nervous. I have cares on my mind, and, though my daughter does not realize it, I often lie awake at her side, longing for space to breathe in and freedom to move as freely as my uneasiness demands. Last night my feelings were too much for my self-control, and I arose. I hope I did not seriously disturb you, or awaken anybody, with my restless pacing up and down the hall."

I assured her that it took more than this to disturb me, and that after quieting her daughter I had immediately fallen asleep; all of which she may have believed or may not; I had no means of reading her mind, as she had no means of reading mine.

But whether she was deceived or whether she was not, she certainly looked relieved, and after some short remarks about the weather, turned from me with the most cheerful air in the world, to greet her daughter.

As for me, I have made up my mind to change my room. I shall not say anything about it or make any fuss on the subject, but to-night, and for some nights to come, I intend to take up my abode in a certain small room in the west wing, not very far removed from the dreadful oak parlor.

CHAPTER XX

THE STONE IN THE GARDEN

OCTOBER 11, 1791.

This morning the post brought two letters for my strange guests. Being anxious to see how they would be received, I carried them up to Madame Letellier's room myself.

The ladies were sitting together, the daughter embroidering. At the sight of the letters in my hand they both rose, the daughter reaching me first.

"Let me have them!" she cried, a glad, bright color showing for a moment on her cheek.

"From your father?" asked the mother, in a tone of nonchalance that did not deceive me.

The girl shook her head. A smile as exquisite as it was sad made her mouth beautiful. "From—" she began, but stopped, whether from an instinct of maidenly shame or some secret signal from her mother, I cannot say.

"Well, never mind," the mother exclaimed, and turned away toward the window in a manner that gave me my dismissal.

So I went out, having learned nothing, save the fact that mademoiselle had a lover, and that her lips could smile.

They did not smile again, however. Next day she looked whiter than ever, and languid as a broken blossom.

"She is ill," declared madame. "The stairs she has to climb are too much for her."

"Ah, ha!" thought I to myself. "That is the first move," and waited for the next development.

It has not come as soon as I expected. Two days have passed, and though Mademoiselle Letellier grows paler and thinner, nothing more has been said about the stairs. But the time has not passed without its incident, and a serious enough one, too, if these women are, as I fear, in the secret of the hidden chamber.

It is this: In the garden is a white stone. It is plain-finished but unlettered. It marks the resting-place of Honora Urquhart. For reasons which we all thought good, we have taken no uninterested person into the secret of this grave, any more than we have into that of the hidden chamber.

Consequently no one in the house but myself could answer Madame Letellier, when, stopping in her short walk up and down the garden path, she asked what the white stone meant and what it marked. I would not answer her. I had seen from the window where I stood the quick surprise with which she had come to a standstill at the sight of this stone, and I had caught the tremble in her usually steady voice as she made the inquiry I have mentioned above. I therefore hastened down and joined her before she had left the spot.

"You are wondering what this stone means," I observed, with an indifferent tone calculated to set her at her ease. Then suddenly, and with a changed voice and a secret look into her face, I added: "It is a headstone; a dead body lies here."

She quivered, and her lids fell. For all her self-possession—and she is the most self-possessed person I ever saw in my life—she showed a change that gave me new thoughts and made me summon up all the strength I am mistress of, in order to preserve the composure which her agitation had so deeply shaken.

"You shock me," were her first words, uttered very slowly, and with a transparent show of indifference. "It is not usual to find a garden used for a burial place. May I ask whose body lies here? That of some faithful black or of a favorite horse?"

"It is not that of a horse," I returned, calmly. And greatly pleased to find that I had placed her in a position where she would be obliged to press the question if she would learn anything more, I walked slowly on, convinced that she would follow me.

She did, giving me short side glances, which I bore with an equanimity that much belied the tempest of doubt, repugnance and horror that were struggling blindly in my breast. But she did not renew the subject of the grave. Instead of that, she opened one of her most fascinating conversations, endeavoring by her wiles and graces to get at my confidence and insure my good will.

And I was hypocrite enough to deceive her into thinking she had done so. Though I showed her no great warmth, I carefully restrained myself from betraying my real feelings, allowing her to talk on, and giving her now and then an encouraging word or an inviting smile.

For I felt that she was a serpent and must be met as such. If she were the woman I thought her, I should gain nothing and lose all by betraying my distrust, while if she felt me to be her dupe I might yet light upon the secret of her interest in the oak parlor.

Her daughter was waiting for us in the doorway when we reached the house. At the sight of her pure face, with its tender gray eyes and faultless features, a strong revulsion seized me, and I found it difficult not to raise my arms in protest between her beauty and winning womanliness and the subtile and treacherous-hearted being who glided so smoothly toward her. But the movement, had I made it, would have been in vain. At the sight of each other's faces a lovely smile arose on the daughter's lips, while on the mother's flashed a look of love which would be unmistakable even on the countenance of a tiger, and which was at this moment so vivid and so real that I never doubted again, if I had ever doubted before, that mademoiselle was her own child—flesh of her flesh, and bone of her bone.

"Ah, mamma," cried one soft voice, "I have been so lonesome!"

"Darling," returned the other, in tones as true and caressing, "I will not leave you again, even for a walk, till you are quite well." And taking her by the waist, she led her down the hall toward the stairs, looking back at me as she did so, and saying: "I cannot take her to Albany until she is better. You must think what we can do to make her strong again, Mrs. Truax." And she sighed as she looked up the short flight of stairs her daughter had to climb.

OCTOBER 15, 1791.

That stone in the garden seems to possess a magnetic attraction for madame. She is over it or near it half the time. If I go out in the early morning to gather grapes for dinner, there she is before me, pacing up and down the paths converging to that spot, and gazing with eager eyes at that simple stone, as if by the force of her will she would extract its secret and make it tell her what she evidently burns to know. If I want flowers for the parlor mantel, and hurry into the garden during the heat of the day, there is madame with a huge hat on her head, plucking asters or pulling down apples from the low-hanging branches of the trees. It is the same at nightfall. Suspicious, always suspicious now, I frequently stop, in passing through the upper western hall, to take a peep from the one window that overlooks this part of the garden. I invariably see her there; and remembering that her daughter is ill, remembering that in my hearing she promised that daughter that she would not leave her again, I feel impelled at times to remind her of the fact, and see what reply will follow. But I know. She will say that she is not well herself; that the breeze from the river does her good; that she loves nature, and sleeps better after a ramble under the stars. I cannot disconcert her—not for long—and I cannot compete with her in volubility and conversational address, so I will continue to play a discreet part and wait.

OCTOBER 17, 1791.

Madame has become bolder, or her curiosity more impatient. Hitherto she has been content with haunting the garden, and walking over and about that one place in it which possesses peculiar interest for her and me. But this evening, when she thought no one was looking, when after a hurried survey of the house and grounds she failed to detect my sharp eyes behind the curtain of the upper window, she threw aside discretion, knelt down on the sod of that grave, and pushed aside the grass that grows about the stone, doubtless to see if there was any marks or inscription upon it. There are none, but I determined she should not be sure of this, so before she could satisfy herself, I threw up the window behind which I stood, making so much noise that it alarmed her, and she hastily rose.

I met her hasty look with a smile which it was too dark for her to see, and a cheerful good evening which I presume fell with anything but a cheerful sound upon her ears.

"It is a lovely evening," I cried. "Have you been admiring the sunset?"

"Ah, so much!" was her quick reply, and she began to saunter in slowly. But I knew she left her thoughts out there with that mysterious grave.

12 M.

Another midnight adventure! Late as it is, I must put it down, for I cannot sleep, and to-morrow will bring its own story.

I had gone to bed, but not to sleep. The anxieties under which I now labor, the sense of mystery which pervades the whole house, and the secret but ever-present apprehension of some impending catastrophe, which has followed me ever since these women came into the house, lay heavily on my mind, and prevented all rest. The change of room may also have added to my disturbance. I am wedded to old things, old ways, and habitual surroundings. I was not at home in this small and stuffy apartment, with its one narrow window and wretched accommodations. Nor could I forget near what it lay, nor rid myself of the horror which its walls gave me whenever I realized, as I invariably did at night, that only a slight partition separated me from the secret chamber, with its ghastly memories and ever to be remembered horrors.

I was lying, then, awake, when some impulse—was it a magnetic one?—caused me to rise and look out of the window. I did not see anything unusual—not at first—and I drew back. But the impulse returned, and I looked again, and this time perceived among the shadows of the trees something stirring in the garden, though what I could not tell, for the night was unusually dark, and my window very poorly situated for seeing.

But that there was something there was enough, and after another vain attempt to satisfy myself as to its character, I dressed and went out into the hall, determined to ascertain if any outlet to the house was open.

I did not take a light, for I know the corridors as I do my own hand. But I almost wished I had as I sped from door to door and window to window; for the events which had blotted my house with mystery were beginning to work upon my mind, and I felt afraid, not of my shadow, for I could not see it, but of my step, and the great gulfs of darkness that were continually opening before my eyes.

However, I did not draw back, and I did not delay. I tried the front door, and found it locked; then the south door, and finally the one in the kitchen. This last was ajar. I knew then what had happened. Madame has had more than one talk with Chloe lately, and the good negress has not been proof against her wiles, and has taught her the secret of the kitchen lock. I shall talk to Chloe to-morrow. But, meantime, I must follow madame.

But should I? I know what she is doing in the garden. She is wandering round and round that grave. If I saw her I could not be any surer of the fact, and I would but reveal my own suspicions to her by showing myself as a spy. No; I will remain here in the shadows of the kitchen, and wait for her to return. The watch may be weird, but no weirder than that of a previous night. Besides, it will not be a long one; the air is too chilly outside for her to risk a lengthy stay in it. I shall soon perceive her dark figure glide in through the doorway.

And I did. Almost before I had withdrawn into my corner I heard the faint fall of feet on the stone without, then the subdued but unmistakable sound of the opening door, and lastly the locking of it and the hasty tread of footsteps as she glided across the brick flagging and disappeared into the hall beyond.

"She has laid the ghost of her unrest for to-night," thought I. "To-morrow it will rise again." And I felt my first movement of pity for her.

Alas! does that unrest spring from premeditated or already accomplished guilt? Whichever it may be—and I am ready to believe in either or both—she is a burdened creature, and the weight of her fears or her intentions lies heavily upon her. But she hides the fact with consummate address, and when under the eyes of people smiles so brightly and conducts herself with such a charming grace that half the guests that come and go consider her as lovely and more captivating than her daughter. What would they think if they could see her as I do rising in the night to roam about a grave, the unmarked head-stone of which baffles her scrutiny?

OCTOBER 18, 1791.

This morning I rose at daybreak, and going into the garden, surveyed the spot which I had imagined traversed by Madame Letellier the night before. I found it slightly trampled, but what interested me a great deal more than this was the fact that, on a certain portion of the surface of the stone I have so often mentioned, there were to be seen small particles of a white substance, which I soon discovered to be wax.

Thus the mystery of her midnight visit is solved. She has been taking an impression of what, in her one short glimpse of yesterday evening, she had thought to be an inscription. What a wonderful woman she is! What skill she shows; what secrecy and what purpose. If she cannot compass her end in one way, she will in another; and I begin to have, notwithstanding my repugnance and fear, a wholesome respect for her ability and the relentless determination which she shows in every action she performs.

When she finds that her wax shows her nothing but the natural excrescences and roughnesses of an unhewn stone, will she persist in her visits to the garden? I think not.

OCTOBER 19, 1791.

My last surmise was a true one. Madame has not spent a half hour all told in the garden since that night. She has turned her attention again to the oak parlor, and soon we shall see her make some decided move in regard to it.

CHAPTER XXI

IN THE OAK PARLOR

OCTOBER 20, 1791.

The long expected move has been made. This morning madame asked me if I had not some room on the ground floor which I could give to her daughter and her in exchange for the one they now occupy. Her daughter had been accustomed to living on one floor, and felt the stairs keenly.

I answered at first—"No." Then I appeared to bethink me, and told her, with seeming reluctance, that there was one room below which I sometimes opened to guests, but that just now it was in such a state of dilapidation I had shut it up till I could find the opportunity of repairing it.

"Oh!" she replied, subduing her eagerness to the proper point, "you need not wait for that. We are not particular persons. Only let me see the roses come back to my daughter's cheeks, and I can bear any amount of discomfort. Where is this room?"

I pretended not to hear her.

"It would take two days to get it into any sort of condition fit for sleeping in," I murmured reflectively. "The floor is so loose in places that you cannot walk across it without danger of falling through. Then there is the chimney—"

She was standing near me and I heard her draw her breath quickly, but she gave no other sign of emotion, not even in the sound of her voice as she interrupted me with the words:

"Oh! if you have got to make the room all over, we might as well not consider the subject. But I am sure it is not necessary. Do let me see it, and I can soon tell you whether we can be comfortable there or not."

I had sworn to myself never to enter that room again, but such oaths are easily broken. Leaving her for a moment, I procured my key, and taking her with me down the west hall, I unlocked the fatal door and bade her enter.

She hesitated for an instant, but only for an instant. Then she walked coolly in, and stood waiting while I crossed the floor to the window and threw it open. Her first glance flashed to the mantel and its adjacent wainscoting; then, finding everything satisfactory in that direction, it flew over the desolate walls and stiff, high-backed chairs, till it rested on the bare four-poster, denuded of its curtains and coverlets.

"A gloomy place!" she declared; "but you can easily make it look inviting with fresh curtains and a cheerful fire. I am sure that, dismal as it is, it will be more welcome to my daughter than the sunny room up stairs. Besides, the window looks out on the river, and that is always interesting. You will let us come here, will you not? I am sure, if we are willing, you ought to be."

I gasped inwardly, and agreed with her. Yet I made a few more objections. But as I intended that she should sleep in this room, I finally cleared my brow, and announced that the room should be ready for her occupancy on Friday; and with this she had to be content.

OCTOBER 21.

Bless God that I am mistress in my own house! I can order, I can have performed whatever I choose, without fuss, without noise, and without gossip. This is very fortunate just now, for while I am openly having the floor mended in the oak parlor, I am secretly having another piece of work done, which, if once known, would arouse suspicions and awaken conjectures that would destroy all my plans concerning the mysterious guests who insist upon inhabiting the accursed oak parlor.

What this work is can be best understood by a glance at the accompanying diagram, which is a copy of the one drawn up by the Englishman for Mr. Tamworth.

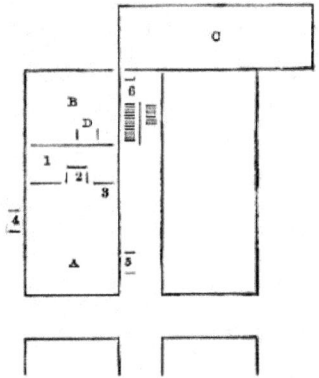

1—Secret chamber.
2—Fire-place.
3—Secret spring.
4—Garden window.
5—Door to oak parlor.
6—Clock on stairs to second story.
Entrance to room B under stairway.

Here you see that the secret chamber lies between the rooms A and B. A is the parlor and B is the small room in which I had put up my bed after the nocturnal adventure of October 10. It has always been used as a store room until now, and as no one handles the keys of this house but myself, the fact of my using it for any other purpose is known only to Margery and a certain quiet and reticent workman from Cruger's shop, to whom I have intrusted the task of opening a passage at D through the wall. For I must have proper means of communication with this room before I can allow Madame Letellier and her daughter to take up their abode in it. Though the former's plans are a mystery to me; though I feel that she loves her daughter, and, therefore, cannot meditate evil against her, still my doubts of her are so great that I must know her intentions, if possible, and to do this I contemplate keeping a watch over that den of wicked memories which will be at once both unsuspected and vigilant.

The flooring of the parlor is nearly completed, and to-night will see the door of communication between my room and the secret chamber hung and ready for use.

OCTOBER 22.

A month ago, if any one had told me that I would not only walk of my own free will into the secret chamber, but take up my abode in it, eat in it and sleep in it, I would have said that person was mad. And yet this is just what I have done.

The result of my first vigil was unexpected. I had looked for—well, I hardly know what I did look for. My anticipations were vague, but they did not lead me in the right direction. But let me tell the story. After I had installed my guests in their new apartment, I informed them that I would have to say good-by for a season, as I had an affection of the eyes—which was true enough—which at times compelled me to shut myself up in a dark room and forego all company. That I felt one of these spells coming on—which was not true—and that by a speedy resort to darkness and quiet, I hoped to prevent the attack from reaching its usual point of distress. Mademoiselle Letellier looked disappointed, but madame ill disguised her relief and satisfaction. Convinced now beyond all doubt that she had some plan in mind which made her dread my watchfulness, I made such final arrangements as were necessary, and betook myself at once to my new room. Once there, I moved immediately into the dark chamber, and walking with the utmost circumspection, crossed to the wall adjoining the oak parlor, and laying my ear against the opening into that room, I listened.

At first I heard nothing, probably because its inmates were still. Then I caught an exclamation of weariness, and soon some words of desultory conversation. Relieved beyond expression, not only because I could hear, but because they talked in English, I withdrew again into my own room. The most difficult problem in the world was solved. I had found the means by which I could insinuate myself, unseen and unsuspected, into the secret confidences of two women, at moments when they felt themselves alone and at the mercy of no judgment but that of God. Should I learn enough to pay me for the humiliation of my position? I did not weary myself by questioning. I knew my motive was pure, and fixed my mind upon that.

Several times before the day was over did I return to the secret chamber and bend my ear to the wall. But in no instance did I linger long, for if the two ladies spoke at all it was on trivial subjects, and in such tones as indicated that neither their passions nor any particular interests were engaged. For such talk I had no ear.

"It will not be always so," I thought to myself. "When night comes and the heart opens, they will speak of what lies upon their minds."

And so it happened. As the inn grew quiet and the lights began to disappear from the windows, I crept again to my station against the partition, and in a darkness and atmosphere that at any other time in my life would have completely unnerved me, hearkened to the conversation within.

"Oh, mamma," were the first words I heard, uttered in English, as all their talk was when they were moved or excited, "if you would only explain! If you would only tell me why you do not wish me to receive letters from him! But this silence—this love and this silence are killing me. I cannot bear it. I feel like a lost child who hears its mother's voice in the darkness, but does not know how to follow that voice to the refuge it bespeaks."

"Time was when daughters found it sufficient to know that their parents disapproved of an act, without inquiring into their reasons for it. Your father has told you that the marquis is not eligible as a husband for you, and he expects this to content you. Have I the right to say more than he?"

"Not the right, perhaps, mamma. I do not appeal to your sense of right, but to your love. I am very unhappy. My whole life's peace is trembling in the balance. You ought to see it—you do see it—yet you let me suffer without giving me one reason why I should do so."

The mother's voice was still.

"You see!" the daughter went on again, after what seemed like a moment of helpless waiting. "Though my arms are about you, and my cheek pressed close to yours, you will not speak. Do you wonder that I am heart-broken—that I feel like turning my face to the wall and never looking up again?"

"I wonder at nothing."

Was that madame's voice? What boundless misery! what unfathomable passion! what hopeless despair!

"If he were unworthy!" her daughter here exclaimed.

"It you could point to anything he lacks. But he has wealth, a noble name, a face so handsome that I have seen both you and papa look at him in admiration; and as for his mind and attainments, are they not superior to those of all the young men who have ever visited us? Mamma, mamma, you are so good that you require perfection in a son-in-law. But is he not as near it as a man may be? Tell me, darling, for in my dreams he always seems so."

I heard the answer, though it came slowly and with apparent effort.

"The marquis is an admirable young man, but we have another suitor in mind whose cause we more favor. We wish you to marry Armand Thierry."

"A shop-keeper and a revolutionist! Oh, mamma!"

"That is why we brought you away. That is why you are here—that you might have opportunity to bethink yourself, and learn that the parents' views in these matters are the truest ones, and that where we make choice, there you must plight your troth. I assure you that our reasons are good ones, if we do not give them. It is not from tyranny—"

Here the set, strained voice stopped, and a sudden movement in the room beyond showed that the mother had risen. In fact, I presently heard her steps pacing up and down the floor.

"I know it is not tyranny," the daughter finished, in the soft tones that were so great a contrast to her mother's. "Tyranny I could have understood; but it is mystery, and that is not so easily comprehended. Why should you and papa be mysterious? What is there in our simple life to create secrecy between persons who love each other so dearly? I see nothing, know nothing; and yet—"

"Honora!"

The word struck me like a blow. "Honora!" Great heaven! was that the name of this young girl?

"You are giving too free range to your imagination. You—"

I did not hear the rest. I was thinking of the name I had just heard, and wondering if my suspicions were at fault. They would never have called their child Honora. Who were these women, then? Friends of the Dudleighs? Avengers of the dead? I glued my ear still closer to the wall.

"We have cherished you." The mother was still speaking. "We have given you all you craved, and more than you asked. From the moment you were born we have both lavished all the tenderness of our hearts upon you. And all we ask in return is trust." The hard voice, hard because of emotion, I truly believe, quavered a little over that word, but spoke it and went on. "What we do for you now, as always, is for your best good. Will you not believe it, Honora?"

The last appeal was uttered in a passionate tone. It seemed to move the daughter, for her voice had a sob in it as she replied:

"Yes; yes; but why not enlighten me as to your reasons for a course so remarkable? Most parents desire their daughters to do well, but you, on the contrary, not only wish, but urge me to do ill. A noble lover sues for my hand, and his cause is slighted; an ignoble one requests the same favor, and you run to grant it. Is there love in this? Is there consideration? Perhaps; but if so, you should be able to show where it lies. I am not a child, young as I am; I will understand any reasons you may advance. Then let me have your confidence; it is all I ask, and surely it is not much, when you see how I suffer from my disappointment."

The restless steps ceased. I heard a groan close to my ear; the mother was evidently suffering frightfully.

"Papa is prosperous," the daughter pleadingly continued. "I know your decision cannot be the result of financial difficulties. And then, if it were, the marquis is rich, and—"

"Honora!"—the mother had turned. I heard her advance toward her daughter—"do you really love the marquis? You have seen him but a few times, have held hardly any intercourse with him, and at your age fancy often takes the place of love. You do not love him, Honora, my child; you cannot; you will forget—"

"Oh, mamma! Oh, mamma! Oh, mamma!"

The tone was enough. Silence reigned, broken at last by Mademoiselle Letellier saying: "It is not necessary to see such a man as he is very many times in order to adjudge him to be the best and noblest that the world contains. But, mamma, you are not correct in saying that I scarcely know him. Though you will not be frank with me, I am going to be frank with you and tell you something that I have hitherto kept closely buried in my breast. I did not think I should ever speak of it to any one, not even to you. Some dreams are so sweet to brood upon alone. But the shadow which your silence has caused to fall between us has taught me the value of openness and truth. I shall never hide anything from you again; so listen, sweet mamma, while I open to you my heart, and learn, as you can only learn from me, how your Honora first came to know and appreciate the Marquis de la Roche-Guyon."

"Was it not," interrupted the mother, "at the great ball where he was formally introduced to us?"

"No, mamma."

Madame sighed.

"Girls are all alike," she cried. "You think you know them, and lo! there comes a day when you find that it is in a stranger's hand you must look for a key to their natures."

"And is not this what God wills?" suggested the child. "Indeed, indeed, you must blame nature and not me. I did not want to deceive you. I only found it impossible to speak. Besides, if you had looked at me closely enough, you would have seen yourself that I had met the marquis before. Such blushes do not come with a first introduction. I remember their burning heat yet. Are my cheeks warm now? I feel as if they ought to be. But there is nothing to grieve you in these blushes. It is only the way a loving heart takes to speak. There is no wicked shame in them; none, none."

"Oh, God!"

Did the daughter hear that bitter exclamation? She did not appear to; for her voice was quite calm, though immeasurably loving, as she proceeded in these words:

"I was always a mother-girl. From the first day I can remember, I have known nothing sweeter than to sit within reach of your fondling hand. You were always so tender with me, mamma, even when I must have grieved you or disappointed your hopes or your pride. If I were in the way I never saw it, nor can I remember, of all the looks which have sometimes puzzled me in your face, one that spoke of impatience or lack of sympathy with my pleasures or my griefs. With papa it was not always so. No; don't stop me. You must let me speak of him. Though he has never been unkind to me, he has a way of frowning at times that frightens me. Whether he is displeased or simply ill I cannot say, but I have always felt a dread of papa's presence which I never felt of yours; and yet you frown, too, at times, though never upon me, mamma, dear—never upon me."

A pause that was filled in by a kiss, and then the tender voice went on:

"You can imagine, then, what a turmoil was aroused in my breast when one day, while leaning from the window, I saw a face in the street below that awakened within me such strange feelings I could not communicate them even to my mother. I who had hitherto confessed to her every trivial emotion of my life, shrank in a moment, as it were, from revealing a secret no deeper than that I had looked for one half minute upon the form of a passing stranger, and in that minute learned more of my own heart and of the true meaning of life than in all the sixteen years I had hitherto lived. You have seen him since, and you know he possesses every grace that can render a man attractive; but to me that day he did not look like a man at all, or if I thought of him as such, I thought of him as one who set a pattern to his fellows, while retaining his own immeasurable superiority. He did not see me. I do not know that I wished him to. I was quite content to watch him from where I stood, and note his lordly walk and kindly mien, and dream—oh, what did I dream that day! The memory of your own girlhood must tell you, mamma. I did not know his name; I did not suspect his rank; but from his youth I judged him to be single, from his bearing I knew him to be noble, and from his look, which called out a reflected brightness on every face he chanced to pass, I was assured that he was happy and that he was good. And what does a girl's fancy need more? Still a glimpse so short might not have had such deep consequences if it had not been followed by an event which rendered those first impressions indelible."

"An event, Honora?"

"Yes, mamma. You remember the day you sent me with Cecile to take my first lessons in tambour work of Madame Douay?"

"Remember? Oh, my child, that awful day when you came near losing your life! When the house fell with you in it, and—"

"Yes, yes, mamma, and I came home looking so pale you thought I was hurt, and fainted away, and would have died yourself if I had not kissed you back to life. Well, mamma, dear, I was hurt, but not in my body. It was my heart that had received a wound—a wound from which I never shall recover, for it was made by the greatness, the goodness, the noble self-sacrifice of the marquis."

"Honora! And you never mentioned his name—never!"

"I know, I know, mamma; but you have already forgiven me for that. You know it was from no unworthy motive. Think how you felt when you first saw papa. Think—"

A hurried movement from the mother interrupted her.

"Do not keep me in suspense," she pleaded; "let me hear what you have to tell."

"But you are cold; you shudder. Let me get a shawl."

"No, no, child, I am not cold, only impatient. Go on with your story—go on. How came you to meet the marquis in that place?"

"Ah," cried the daughter, "it was a strange occurrence. It all came about through a mistake of Cecile's. Madame Douay, as we were told by the concierge, lived on the fourth floor, but Cecile made a miscount and we went up to the fifth, and as there was a Madame Douay there also, we did not detect our error, but went into her apartments and were seated in the small salon to await madame's presence. We had not told our errand, so we could not blame the maid who admitted us, nor, though madame failed to appear, did we ever remember to blame any one, for presently through the open window near which we sat there came the sound of voices from the room above, and a drama began of such startling interest that we could think of nothing else.

"Two men were talking. Young men they seemed, and though I could not see them, I could tell from the fresh, fine voice of the one that he was a true man, and from the sneering, smothered tones of the other that he was not only a cynic, but of vicious tendencies. The first one was saying, 'I never suspected this,' when my attention was first called to their words, and the answer which came was as follows: 'If you had, I should not have had the pleasure of seeing you here. Men are not apt to rush voluntarily upon their deaths, and that you are a dead man you already know; for I have sworn to kill you as the clock strikes three, and it is but ten minutes of that time, and you have not a weapon with which to defend yourself.'

"Mamma, you can imagine my feelings at hearing these words, though they were uttered by a person I could not see, to another person equally unknown to me? I looked at Cecile and she looked at me, but we could neither of us move. Every faculty seemed paralyzed save that of hearing. We held our breaths and listened for the reply. It came instantly and without a thrill in its clear accents.

"'You are a gentleman, and no common assassin. How can you reconcile such an act as this with your honor, or with what sophistries quiet the stings of your conscience when time shall have shown you the sin of so unprovoked an onslaught?'

"'It is not unprovoked,' was the harsh and bitter reply. 'You promised to marry Mademoiselle de Fontaine, and yesterday, at three o'clock—ah, I was there!—you formally renounced your claims. This is an insult that calls for blood, and blood it shall have. Twenty-four hours have elapsed less ten minutes, since you cast this slur upon a noble lady's good name. When the hour is ripe, you will pay the penalty it requires with your life.'

"'But,' urged his young companion, 'Mademoiselle de Fontaine had herself requested the breaking off of this contract. I am but following the lady's behests in withdrawing from a position forced upon us against our will, and in direct opposition to her happiness.'

"'And by what right do you presume to follow the behests of a lady still under age? Has she not guardians to consult? Should not I—'

"'You?'

"'Pardon me, I have not introduced myself, it seems. I am the Marquis de la Roche-Guyon.'"

Honora paused; her mother's exclamation had stopped her:

"The marquis! Oh! Honora, and you have always said he was so good!"

"Wait, mamma; remember it is the cynical voice which is speaking, and the marquis's voice is not cynical. The words, however, are what I have told you; 'I am the Marquis de la Roche-Guyon.'

"Of course, not knowing either party, nor this name, least of all realizing that it was the one by which the gentleman addressed was himself known, I did not understand why it should create so great an impression. But that it did was evident, not only from the momentary hush that followed, but from the violent exclamation that burst from the young man's lips. 'You scoundrel!' was his cry. But instantly he seemed to regret the word, for he said almost with the same breath: 'Your pardon, but there is but one man in the world besides myself who could, under any circumstances, have a right to that name.'

"'And that man?'

"'Is my cousin, the deceased marquis's son, long esteemed dead also, and now legally accepted as such.'

"'And what assures you that I am not he? Your eyes? Well, I am changed, Louis, but not so changed that a good look should not satisfy you that I am the man I claim to be. Besides, you should know this mark on my forehead. You gave it to me—'

"'Isidor!'

"I could not comprehend it then, but I have learned since that the marquis—our marquis, I mean—had only just come into his title; that the son of the preceding Marquis de la Roche-Guyon had been so long missing that the courts had finally adjudged him dead, and given up his inheritance to his cousin; that the first act of the new marquis was to liberate the Demoiselle de Fontaine from an engagement that stood in the way of her marriage with one more desirable to her; and that the unexpected appearance of the real heir in this sudden and mysterious manner was as great a surprise to him as any mortal circumstance could be. Yet to me, who waited with palpitating heart and anxious ears for what should be said next, there was no evidence of this in his tone. With the politeness we are accustomed to in Frenchmen he observed:

"'You are welcome, Isidor;' and then, as if struck himself by the incongruity between this phrase and the look and manner of his companion, he added, in slow tones—'even if you do bring a sword with you.'

"The other, the real marquis, as I suppose, seemed to hesitate at this, and I began to hope he was ashamed of his dreadful threats and would speedily beg the other's pardon. But I did not know the man, or realize the determination which lay at the bottom of his furious and uncompromising words. But he soon made it evident to us.

"'Louis,' he exclaimed, 'you have always been my evil genius. From our childhood you have stood in my way with your superior strength, beauty, prowess and address. When I was young I simply shrank from you in shame and distaste, but as I grew older I learned to detest you; and now that I see you again, after five years of absence, handsome as ever, taller than ever, and radiant, notwithstanding your nearness to death, with memories such as I have never known, nor can know, and beliefs such as I have never cherished nor will cherish, I hate you so that I find it difficult to wait for the five minutes yet to elapse before my word will let me lift my pistol and fire upon you.'

"'Then it is your hate of me, and not your fondness for your sister, that has led you to lay this trap for me?' exclaimed the other. 'I should think your hate would be satisfied by the change which your return will make in my prospects. From the marquisate of La Roche-Guyon to a simple captaincy in his majesty's guards is quite a step, Isidor. Will it not suffice to soothe an antagonism which I never shared?'

"'Nothing can soothe it, not even your death! You have robbed me of too much. First, of the world's esteem, then of my mother's confidence, and, lastly, of my father's love. Yes; deny it if you will, my father loved you better than he did me. This was the reason he sent me from home; and when, shipwrecked and captured by savages, I found myself thrown into an Eastern dungeon, half my misery and all my rage were in the thought that he would not consider my loss a misfortune, but die in greater peace and hope from knowing that his family honors would devolve upon one more after his own heart than myself. Oh! I have had cause, and I have had time to nourish my hate. Five years in a dungeon affords one leisure, and on every square stone of that wall, and upon every inch of its relentless pavement, I have beaten out this determination with my bare hands and manacled feet, that if I ever did escape, and ever did return to the home of my fathers, I would have full pay for the suffering you have caused me, even if I had it in your blood. I have returned, and I find my father dead, and in his place yourself, happy, insolent, and triumphant. Can you blame me for remembering my vows, for resenting what will ever seem an insult to my sister, and for wishing to hurry the time that moves so slowly toward the fatal stroke of three?'

"'I do not blame you, because you are a madman. I do not fear you, because, having no one in the world to love, I do not greatly dread a sudden release from it. But I pity you because you have suffered, and will defend myself because your sufferings will be increased rather than diminished by the success of your crazy intentions.'

"The answer came, quick and furious:

"'I do not want your pity, and I scorn any defense which you can make. Do you think I have not made my calculations well? There is nothing here which can give you hope. We are alone on the sixth story. Beneath us are only women, and if you call from the window, I can shoot you dead before your voice can reach the street. Perhaps, though, you do not think of saving yourself, but of ensnaring me. Bah! as if the sight of the headsman would stop me now. Besides, I am prepared for flight. Have you looked at this house? It is not like other houses; it is double, and the room in which we stand has other foundations and walls from this one behind me which I guard with my pistol. Let the deed be once done—and the clock, as you see, gives us but one minute more—and I leap into this other apartment, down another flight of stairs from those you came up, and so to another door that opens upon another street. Then shout, if you will; I am safe. As to your life, it is as much at my command as if my bullet were already in your heart.'

"'We will see!' was the thundering reply, and with these words a rush was made that shook the floor above our heads, and scattered bits of plaster down upon us. Released by the action from the fearful spell which had benumbed my limbs, I felt that I could move at last, and, leaping to my feet, I uttered scream after scream. But they perished in my throat, smothered by a new fear; for at this moment my arm was caught by Cecile, and following, with horrified gaze, the pointing of her uplifted hand, I saw the straight line of the window-ledge before me dip and curve, and yielding to the force of her agonized strength, I let myself be dragged across the floor, while before us, beneath us, above us, all was one chaos of heaving and crashing timbers, which, in another instant, broke into a thunder of confused sounds, and we beheld beneath us a pit of darkness, death, and tumult, where, but an instant before, were all the appurtenances of a comfortable and luxurious home.

"We were safe, for we had reached the flooring of the second house before that of the first had completely fallen, but I could not think of myself, narrow as my escape had been, and marvelous as was the warning which had revealed to Cecile the only path of safety. For in the clouded space above me, overhanging a gulf I dared not measure with my eyes or sound with my imagination, I saw clinging by one arm to a beam the awful figure of a man, while crouching near him on a portion of flooring that still clung intact to the wall, I beheld another in whose noble traits, distorted though they were by the emotions of the moment, I recognized him who, but a month before, had changed the world for me with his look.

"Ah! mamma, and a thousand deaths lay between us; and we could neither reach him nor give any alarm, for the space in which we found ourselves was small and shut from the outer world by a door which was locked. How it became locked I never knew, but I have thought that the maid in flying might have turned the key behind her, under some wild impression that by this means she would shut out destruction. However that may be, we were helpless and threatened by death. But our own situation did not alarm us, for theirs was so much more terrible, especially that of the man whose straining arm clung so frantically to a support that threatened every moment to slip from his grasp. I could not look at him, and scarcely could I look at the other. But I did, for in his face there was such a high and noble resolve that it made me forget his danger, till suddenly I heard him speak high above the sounds that arose in a tempest from the street:

"'Do not despair, Isidor. I think I can reach you and pull you up upon the beam. You shall not die a dog's death if I can help it. Hold on and I will come.' And he began to move and raise himself upon the narrow platform on which he stood, and I saw that he meant what he said, and involuntarily and with but little reason I cried:

"'Don't do it! He is your enemy. Save yourself; he is but a murderer; let him go.'

"I said that; I who never had a cruel thought before in my life. But he, without looking to see whence this voice came, answered boldly:

"'It is because he is my enemy that I wish to save him. I could never enjoy a safety won at the expense of his death. Isidor, you must live! So hold on, my cousin.'

"And without saying anything further, this brave man set about a task that seemed to me at that moment not only superhuman but impossible. Gathering himself up, he prepared to make a spring, and in another instant would have launched himself toward that rocking beam, if Cecile, driven to extremity by the slow tottering of the floor upon which we stood, had not shrieked:

"'And to save him you would leave us to perish?'

"He paused and gave one look. 'Yes!' he cried. 'God help you, but you look like innocent women, while he—' The leap was made. He lay clinging to the beam. His cousin, who had not fallen, cast one glance up; their eyes met, and Isidor, as he was called, gave one great sob. 'Oh, Louis!' he murmured, and was silent.

"And then, mamma, there began a struggle for rescue such as I dare not even recall. I saw it because I could not look elsewhere, but I crushed its meaning from my consciousness, lest I should myself perish before I saw him safe. And all the while the figure hanging over us swayed with the rocking of the beam, and gave no help until that last terrible moment when his cousin, reaching down, was able to sustain him under the arm till he could get his other hand up and clasp it around the beam. Then it all looked well, and we began to hope, when suddenly and without warning the nearly rescued man gave a great shriek, and crying, 'You have conquered!' unloosed his grasp, and fell headlong into the abyss.

"Mamma, I did not faint. An unnatural strength seemed given to me. But I looked at the marquis, and for the first time he looked at me, and I saw the expression of horrified amaze with which he had beheld his cousin disappear gradually change to one of the softest and divinest looks that ever visited a noble visage, and knew that even out of that pit of death love had arisen for us two, and that henceforth we belonged to each other, whether our span of life should be cut short in a moment or extended into an eternity of years. His own heart seemed to assure him of the same sweet fact, for the next moment he was renewing his superhuman efforts, but this time for our rescue and his own. He worked himself along that beam; he gave another leap; he landed at our side, and tore a way for us through that closed door. In another five minutes we were in the street, with half Paris surging about us, but before the crowd had quite seized upon me, he had found time to whisper in my ear:

"'I am the Marquis de la Roche-Guyon. It will always be a matter of thankfulness to me that I was not left to sacrifice the fairest woman in the world to the rescue of a thankless coward.'

"Mamma, do you blame me for giving such a man my heart, and do you wonder that what I have dedicated to this hero I can never yield to any other man?"

The mother was silent—for a long time silent. Was she horror-stricken at the story of a danger she had never fully comprehended till now? Or were her thoughts busy with her own past, and its possible incommunicable secrets of blood and horror? The cry she gave at last betrayed anguish, but did not answer this question.

"My child! my child! my child!" That was all, but it seemed torn from her heart, that bled after it.

"He was not long in seeking me out, mamma, dear. With grace and consideration he paid me his court, and I was happy till I saw that you and papa frowned upon an alliance that to me seemed laden with promise. I could not understand it, nor could I understand our hurried departure from France, nor our secret journey here. All has been a mystery to me; but your will is my will, and I dare not complain."

"Pure heart!" broke from the mother's lips. "Would to God—"

"What, dear mamma?"

"That you had been moved by a lesser man than the Marquis de la Roche-Guyon."

"A lesser man?"

"With Armand Thierry, since he is the one you will have to marry."

"I shall not marry him."

"Shall not?"

"If I cannot give my hand where my heart is, I remain unmarried. I dishonor no man with unmeaning marriage vows."

"Honora!"

"I may never be happy, but I will never be base. You yourself cannot wish me to be that. You, who married for love, must understand that a woman loses her title to respect when she utters vows to one man while her heart is with another."

"But—"

"You did marry for love, didn't you, sweet mamma? I like to think so. I like to think that papa never cared for any other woman in all the world but you, and that from the moment you first saw him, you knew him to be the one man capable of rousing every noble instinct within you. It is so sweet to enshrine you in such a pure romance, mamma. Though you have been married sixteen years—ah, how old I am!—I see you sit and look at papa sometimes, for a long, long time without speaking, and though you do not smile, I think, 'She is dreaming of the days when life was pure joy, because it was pure love,' and I long to ask you to tell me about those days, because I am sure, if you did, you would tell me the sweetest story of mutual love and devotion. Isn't it so, mamma mine?"

Would that mother answer? Could she? I seemed to behold her figure pausing petrified in the darkness, drawing deep breaths, and scarcely knowing whether to curse or pray. I listened and listened, but it was long before the answer came. Then it was short and hurried, like the pants of one dying.

"Honora, you hurt me." Another silence. "You make my task too hard. If I know what love is—" She found it hard to go on; but she did—"all the more anguish it must cost me to deny you what is so deeply desired. I—I would make you happy if I could. I will make you happy if it is in my power to do so, but I can hold out no hope—none, none."

"Nor tell me why?"

"Nor tell you why."

"Mamma, you suffer. I see it now, and somehow it makes it easier for me to bear my own suffering. You do not willfully deny me what is as much as my life to me."

"Willfully! Honora! Listen." The mother had stopped in her walk, for I heard her restless tread no more. "You say that I suffer, child. I have never had one happy day. Whatever romance you have woven about me, I have never known, from the hour of my birth till now, one moment of such delight as you experienced when you saw the character of the marquis unfold before you so grandly. The nearest I have ever come to bliss was when you were first placed in my arms. Then, indeed, for one wild moment, I felt the baptism of true love. I looked at you, and my heart opened. Alas! it was to take in pain as well as joy. You had the face— Oh, Heaven! what am I saying? This darkness unnerves me, Honora. Let us have light, light, anything to keep my reason from faltering."

"Mother, mother, you are ill!"

"No. I am simply weak. I always am when I recall your birth and the first few days that followed it. I was so glad to have something I could really love; so glad to feel that my heart beat, and to know that it beat for one so innocent, so sweet, so helpless as yourself. What if I had pains and hours of darkness, did I not have your smile, also, and, later on, your love? Child, if there has been any good in my life—and sometimes I have thought there was a little—it came from you. So, never even question again if I could hurt you willfully. I not only could not do this and live, but to save you from pain I would dare— What would I not dare? Let man or angels say."

Before such passion as this young Honora sank helpless.

"Oh, mamma, mamma," she moaned, "forgive me. I did not know—how could I know? Don't sob, mamma, dear; let me hold you—so; now lay your cheek against mine and simply love me. I will lie quite still and ask no questions, and you will rest, too; and God will bless us, as he always blesses the loving and the true."

But madame did not comply with this endearing request. Satisfying her daughter with a few kisses and some words that the paroxysm of her grief was past, she resumed her walk up and down the room, pausing every now and then as if to listen, and hastily resuming her walk as some slight exclamation from the bed assured her that mademoiselle was not yet asleep. As these pauses always took place when she was near the wall behind which I crouched, I frequently heard her breath, which came heavily, and once the rustle of her gown. But I did not stir. As long as her uneasy form flitted about the room, I clung to the partition, listening, determined that nothing should move me—not even my own terrors. And though night presently merged into midnight, and the silence and horror of the spot became frightful, I kept my post, for the stealthy tread continued, and so did the desultory scraps of conversation, which proved that, if the mother was waiting for the daughter to sleep, the daughter was equally waiting for the mother to retire. And so daylight came, and with it exhaustion to more than one of us three watchers.

And this is the record of the first night spent by me in the secret chamber.

CHAPTER XXII

A SURPRISE FOR HONORA

OCTOBER 22, 1791.

Events crowd. This morning the one girl I have taken into my confidence came to my room with a strange tale. A stranger had arrived, an elegant young gentleman of foreign appearance, who had not yet given his name, but who must be a person of importance, if bearing and address go for anything. He came on horseback, attended by his valet, and his first word, after some directions in regard to his horse, was a request to see the landlady. When told she was ill, he asked for the clerk, and to him was about to put some question, when an exclamation from the doorway interrupted them. Turning, they saw madame standing there, her face petrified into an expression of terrified surprise.

"Mrs.—"

"Hush!" sprang from the lady's lips before he could finish his exclamation; and advancing, she laid her hand on his arm, saying, in French, which, by the way, my clerk understands: "If you hope anything from us, do not speak the name that is faltering on your tongue. For reasons of our own, for reasons of a purely domestic nature, we are traveling incognito. Let me ask you as a gentleman to humor our whim, and to know us at present as Madame and Mademoiselle Letellier."

He bowed, but flushed with embarrassment.

"And mademoiselle? She is well, I trust?"

"Quite well."

"And yourself?"

"Quite well, also. May I ask what has brought you into these parts, whom we thought in another and somewhat distant country?"

"Need you ask?"

They had drawn a little apart by this time, and the clerk heard no more; but their manner—the lady's especially—was so singular that he thought I ought to know that she was here under a false name, and so had sent Margery to me with the news. As for the gentleman and Madame Letellier, they were still conversing in the lowest tones together.

Interested intensely in this new development in the drama hourly unfolding before my eyes, I dismissed Margery with an instruction or two, and passed into the hidden chamber, where I again laid my ear to the wall. The mother would have something to say when she returned, and I determined to hear what it was.

I had to wait a long time, but was rewarded at last by the sound of voices and the distinct exclamation from the daughter's lips:

"Oh, mamma! what has happened?"

The mother's reply was delayed, but it came at last:

"My face is becoming strangely communicative. You will read all my thoughts next. What makes you think anything has happened? Is this a place for occurrences?"

"Oh, mamma! you cannot deceive me. Your very limbs are trembling. See, you can hardly stand; and then, how you look at me! Oh, mamma, dear! is it good news or bad? for from your eyes it might be either. Has he—"

"He, he—always he!" the mother passionately interrupted. "You do not love your mother. You are thinking always of one whom you never saw till a year ago. My doubts, my fears, my sufferings are nothing to you. I might die—"

"Hush! hush! Whenever did you speak like this before, mamma? Love you! Did ever a child love her mother more? But our affection is sure, while that of him you do not like me to mention is threatened, and its existence forbidden. I cannot help but think, mamma, and of him. If I could, I were a traitor to the noblest instincts that sway a woman's heart. I may not marry him—you say I never will—but think of him I must, and pray for him I will, till the last breath has left my lips. So, what is your news, dear mamma? Has papa written?"

"It is too early for the mail."

"True, true. Some one has come, then; a messenger, perhaps, from New York. M. Dubois—"

"Dubois is a traitor. He has not kept the secret of our whereabouts. We have to settle with Monsieur and Madame Dubois, meanwhile—"

"What?"

"Honora, can I trust you?"

"Trust me?"

"Ah! who is trembling now?"

"I! I! But how can I help it! You glance toward the door; you seem afraid some one will come. You—you—"

"Tut! do not mind me! Answer what I ask. Could you see the marquis—talk to him, hear him urge his love and plead for yours, without forgetting that your obedience is mine, and that you are not to give him so much as the encouragement of a glance, till I either give you permission to do so or command from you his immediate and unqualified dismissal?"

"See him?" It was all the poor girl had heard.

"Yes; see him. You have come from Paris—why not he? Since Dubois has proved himself a traitor—"

"Oh, mamma!" came now in great sobs, "you are not playing with me. He has come; he is here; the horse I heard stop at the door—"

"Was that of the marquis," acknowledged the mother. "He is in the sitting room, child, but he does not expect you at present. This evening you shall see him if you will promise me what I have asked. Otherwise he must go. I will have no complications arising out of a secret betrothal. If you have not sufficient strength—"

"Oh, I have strength, mamma! I have strength. Only let me see him, and prove to myself that he is not worn by trouble and suspense, and I will do all you ask of me. Ah, how well I feel! What a beautiful—what a lovely day this is! Must I not go out till evening? May I not take one wee walk in the garden?"

"Not one, my child. At nine o'clock you may go to the sitting room for a half hour. Till then, think over what I have said, and prepare your lips to be dumb and your eyes to remain downcast; for I am firm in my demands, and nothing will make me change them."

"You may trust me." There was despair in the tones now....

As they talked but little after this, and as I was greatly interested in seeing the young man who had been heralded by such glowing descriptions, I stole back to my room, and, putting on a green shade, hastened to join my guests in the front part of the house. One glance from beneath my hurriedly uplifted shade was sufficient to assure me as to which of the gentlemen there assembled was the one I sought. So frank a face, so fine a form, so attractive a manner, were not often seen in my inn, and prepossessed at once in his favor, I advanced to the owner of all these graces, and, calling him by name, bade him welcome to my house.

He must understand our language well, for he immediately turned with gentle urbanity, and discerning, perhaps, something in my face which assured him of my sympathy and respect, entered into a fluent conversation with me that at once increased my admiration and awakened my pity. For I saw that his nature was strong and his feelings deep, and as the future could have nothing but shame and misery, I instinctively felt oppressed by the fate which awaited him.

He did not seem to feel any apprehension himself. His eyes were bright; his smile beaming; his bearing full of hope. Now and then his glance would steal toward the door or through the open windows, as if he longed to catch a glimpse of some passing face or form; and at last, swayed by that sympathy which we women all feel for true love in man or woman, I asked him to accompany me into the garden, promising him a view that would certainly delight him. As the garden was plainly visible from the oak parlor, you can readily understand to what view I alluded. But he had no suspicion of my meaning, and followed me with some reluctance.

But his aspect changed materially when, in walking up and down the paths, I casually remarked:

"This is the least inhabited side of the inn. Only one room is occupied, and that by two foreigners—Madame and Mademoiselle Letellier. Yet it has a pleasant outlook, as you yourself can see."

"Is she—are they behind those windows?" he asked, with an impetuosity I could not but admire in a man with so much to recommend him to the consideration of others. "I beg your pardon," he added, a moment later, after a stolen glance at the house. "I know those ladies, and anything in connection with them is interesting to me."

I believed it, and had hard work to hide my secret trouble. But his preoccupation assisted me, and at length I found courage to remark:

"They are from Paris, I understand. A fine woman, Madame Letellier. Must be much admired in her own land?"

He seemed to have no reason for resenting my curiosity.

"She is," was his quick reply. "She is not only admired, but respected. I have never heard her name mentioned but with honor. I am happy to be known as her friend."

I gave him one quick look. Good God! What lay before this man! And he so unconscious! I felt like wishing the inn would fall to atoms before our eyes, crushing beneath it the sin of the past and his false hopes for the future. He saw nothing. He was smiling upon a rose which he had plucked and was holding in his hand.

"This inn is one of the antiquities," I now observed, anxious to know if any hint of its secrets had ever reached his ears. "They say it is one of the first structures reared on the river. Have you ever heard any of the traditions connected with it?"

"Oh, no," he smiled. "The Happy-Go-Lucky is quite a stranger to me. You cherish up all its legends, though, I have no doubt. Are there any tales of ghosts among them? I can easily imagine certain disembodied spirits wandering through its narrow halls and up and down its winding staircases."

"What spirits?" I asked, convinced, however, by his manner that he was talking at random, with the probable aim of prolonging our walk within view of the window behind which his darling might stand concealed.

"Madame must inform me. I have too little acquaintance with this country to venture among its traditions."

"There is a story," I began; but here a finely modulated but piercing voice rang musically down the paths from the house, and we heard:

"Your eyes will certainly suffer, Mrs. Truax, if you let the hot sun glare upon them so mercilessly." And, turning, we saw madame's smiling face looking from her casement with a meaning that struck us both dumb and led me to shorten our walk lest my interest in the romance then going on should be suspected and my usefulness thus become abridged.

Was it to forestall my suspicions, rid herself of my vigilance, or to insure herself against any forgetfulness on her daughter's part, that madame, some two hours later, sent me the following note:

"DEAR MRS. TRUAX: I can imagine that after your walk in the blazing sunlight you do not feel very well this evening. I must nevertheless request of you a favor, my need being great and you being the only person who can assist me. The Marquis de la Roche-Guyon, with whom I saw you promenading, has come to this place with the express intention of paying court to my daughter. As I am not prepared to frown upon his suit, and equally unprepared to favor it, I do not feel at liberty to refuse him the pleasure of an interview with my daughter, and yet do not desire them to enjoy such an interview alone. As I am ill, quite ill, with a sudden and excruciating attack of pain in my right hip, may I ask if you will fulfill the office of chaperon for me, and, without embarrassment to either party, take such measures as will prevent an absolute confidence between them, till I have obtained the sanction of my husband to an intimacy which I myself dare not encourage?

"Very truly your debtor, if you accomplish this, MADAME LETELLIER."

CHAPTER XXIII

IN THE SECRET CHAMBER

Have only twenty-four hours elapsed? Is it but yesternight that all the terrible events took place, the memory of which are now making my frame tremble? So the clock says, and yet how hard it is to believe it. Madame Letellier— But I will preserve my old method. I will not anticipate events, but relate them as they occurred.

To go back then to the note which I received from madame. I did not like it. I did not see its consistency, and I did not mean to be its dupe. If she intended remaining in the oak parlor, then over the oak parlor I would keep watch; for from her alone breathed whatever danger there might be for any of us, and to her alone did I look for the explanation of her mysterious presence in a spot that should have held a thousand repellent forces for her and hers. As for her sudden illness, that was nonsense. She was as well as I was myself. Had I not seen her standing at the window an hour or two before?

But here I made a mistake. Madame was really ill, as I presently had occasion to observe. For not only was a physician summoned, but word came that she wished to see me, also; and when I went to her room I found her in bed, her face pallid and distorted with pain, and her whole aspect betraying the greatest physical suffering.

It was a rheumatic attack, affecting mainly her right limb, and made her so helpless that, for a moment, I stood aghast at what looked to me like a dispensation of Providence. But in another instant I began to doubt again; for though I knew it was beyond anybody's power to simulate the suffering under which she evidently labored, I was made to feel, by her penetrating and restless looks, that her mind retained its hold upon its purpose, whatever that purpose might be, and that for me to relax my vigilance now would be to give her an advantage that would be immediately seized upon.

I therefore held my sympathies in check; and, while acting the part of the solicitous landlady, watched for that glance or word which should reveal her secret intentions. Her daughter, whose eyes were streaming with tears, stood over her like a pitying angel, and not till we had done all we could to relieve her mother, and subdue her pain, did she allow her longing eyes to turn toward the clock that beat out the passing moments with mechanical precision. It was just a quarter to nine.

The mother saw that glance, and hid her face for a moment; then she took mademoiselle by the hand, and drawing her down to her, whispered audibly:

"I expect you to keep your appointment. Mrs. Truax will send one of the girls to sit with me. Besides, I feel better, and as if I could sleep. Only remember your promise, dear. No look, no hint of your feelings."

Mademoiselle flushed scarlet. Stealing a look at me, she drew back embarrassed, but oh! how joyous. I felt my old heart quiver as I surveyed her, and in spite of the dread form of the redoubtable woman stretched before me, in spite of the grewsome room and its more than grewsome secrets, something of the fairy light of love seemed to fall upon my spirit and lift the darkness from the place for one short and glowing moment.

"Look in the glass," the mother now commanded. "You need to tie up your curls again and to put a fresh flower at your throat. I do not wish you to show weariness. Mrs. Truax"—these words to me in low tones, as her daughter withdrew to the other side of the room—"you received my note?"

I nodded.

"You will do what I ask?"

I nodded again. Deliberate falsehood it was, but I showed no faltering.

"Then I will excuse you now."

I rose.

"And do not send any one to me. I wish to sleep, and another's presence would disturb me. See, the pain is almost gone."

She did look better.

"Your wishes shall be regarded," I assured her. "If you do feel worse, ring this bell and Margery will notify me." And placing the bell rope near her hand, I drew back and presently quitted the room.

Lingering in the hall just long enough to see the lovely Honora flit across the threshold of the sitting-room which I had purposely ordered vacant for her use, I hurried to my room.

It was dark, dark as the secret chamber into which I now stole with the lightest and wariest of steps. Horror, gloom, and apprehension were in the air, which brooded stiflingly in the narrow spot, and had it not been for the righteous purpose sustaining me, I should have fallen at this critical moment, crushed beneath the terrible weight of my own feelings.

But one who has to listen, straining every faculty to catch the purport of what is going on behind an impenetrable wall, soon forgets himself and his own sensations. As I pressed my ear to the wall and caught the sound of a prolonged and painful stir within, I only thought of following the movements of madame, who, I was now sure, had left her bed and was dragging herself, with what difficulty and distress I could but faintly judge by the involuntary groans which now and then left her, across the floor toward the door, the key of which I presently heard turn.

This done, a heavy silence followed, then the slow, dragging sound began again, interrupted now by weary pants and heavy sobs that at first chilled me and then shook me with such fear that it was with difficulty that I could retain my place against the wall. She was crawling in my direction, and at each instant I heard the pants grow louder.

I gradually withdrew, step by step, till I found myself pressed up against the wall in the remotest corner I could find. And here was I standing, enveloped in darkness and dread, when the sounds changed to that of a shuddering, rushing noise which I had heard once before in my life, and from a narrow gap through which the faint light in the room beyond dimly shone in a thread of lesser darkness, the aperture grew, till I could feel rather than see her form, crawling, not walking, through the opening, and hear, distinct enough, her horrible, gurgling tones as she murmured:

"I shall have to grope for what I want—touch it, feel it, for I cannot see. O God! O God! What horror! What punishment!"

Nearer, nearer over the floor she came, dragging her useless limb behind her. Her outstretched arm groped, groped about the floor, while I stood trembling and agonized with horror till her hand touched the skirt of my dress, when, with a great shriek of suddenly liberated feeling, I pushed her from me, and crying out, "Murderess! do you seek the bones of your victim?" I flung open the door against which I stood and let the light from my own room stream in upon us two.

Her face as I saw it at that moment has never left my memory. She had fallen in a heap at my first move, and now lay crushed before me, with only her wide-staring eyes and shaking lips to tell me that she lived.

"You thought I did not know you," I burst forth. "You thought, because I had never seen your face, you could come back here, bringing your innocent daughter with you, and cast yourself into the very atmosphere of your crime without awakening the suspicion of the woman whose house you had made a sepulcher of for so many years. But crime was written too plainly on your brow. The spirit of Honora

Urquhart, breaking the bounds of this room, has walked ever beside you, and I knew you from the first moment that you strayed down this hall."

Broken sounds, unintelligible murmurings, were all that greeted me.

"You are punished," I went on, "in the misery of your daughter. Nemesis has reached you. The blood of Honora Urquhart has called aloud from these walls, and not yourself only, but the still viler being whose name you have so falsely shared, must answer to man and God for the life you so heartlessly sacrificed and the rights you so falsely usurped."

"Mercy!" came in one quick gasp from the crushed heap of humanity before me.

But I was inexorable. I remembered Honora Urquhart's sweet face, and at that moment could think of nothing else. So I went on.

"You have had years of triumph. You have borne your victim's name, worn your victim's clothes, sported with your victim's money. And he, her husband, has looked on and smiled. Day after day, month after month, year after year, you have gone in and out before your friends, unmolested and unafraid; but God's vengeance, though it halts, is sure and keen. Across land and across water the memories of this room have drawn you, and not content with awakening suspicion, you must make suspicion certainty by moving a spring unknown even to myself, and entering this spot, from which the bones of your victim were taken only two months ago, Marah Leighton!"

Moved by the name, she stood up. Tottering and agonized with pain, but firm once more and determined, she towered before me, her face turned toward the room she had left, her hand lifted, her whole attitude that of one listening.

"Hark!" she cried.

It was a knock, a faint, low, trembling knock that we heard, then the word "Mamma" came in muffled accents from the hallway.

A convulsion crossed the countenance of the miserable woman before me.

"Oh, God! my daughter, my daughter!" she cried. And falling at my feet, she groveled in anguish as she pleaded:

"Will you kill her? She knows nothing, suspects nothing. The whole fifteen years of her life are pure. She is a flower. I love her—I love her, though she looks like the woman I hated and killed. She bears her name—why, I do not know—I could not call her anything else; she is my living reproach, and yet I love her. Do you not see it was for her I crossed the water, for her I plunged my living hand into this tomb to learn if our secret had ever been discovered, and if there was any hope that she might yet be made happy? Ah, woman, woman, you are not a wretch—a demon! You will not sentence this innocent soul to disgrace and misery. Even if I must die—and I swear that I will die if you say so—leave to my child her hopes; keep secret my sin, and take the blessing of the most miserable being that crawls upon the earth, as a solace for your old age. Hear me; hear a wretched mother's plea—"

"It is too late," I broke in. "Even were I silent there are others upon your track. I doubt if your husband does not already know that the day of his prosperity is at an end."

She gave a low cry, and tottered from the place. Entering her own room, she threw herself upon the bed. I followed, drawing the curtains about her. Then closing the door of communication between the oak parlor and the chamber beyond, I passed to the door behind which we could yet hear her daughter's soft voice calling, and, unlocking it, let the radiant creature in.

"Oh, mamma!" she began, "I could not keep my word—"

But here I held up my hand, and drawing her softly out, told her that her mother needed rest just now, and that if she would come to my room for a little while it would be best; and so prevailed upon her that she promised to do what I asked, though I saw her cast longing glances through the partly opened door toward the somber bed so like a tomb, and which at that moment was a tomb, had she known it—a tomb of hope, of joy, of peace for evermore.

I was just going out, when a slight stir detained me. Looking back, I saw a hand thrust out from between the falling curtains. Just a hand, but how eloquent it was! Pointing it out to mademoiselle, I said:

"Your mother's hand. Give it a kiss, mademoiselle, but do not part the curtains."

She smiled and crossed to that ominous bed. Kneeling, she kissed the hand, which thereupon raised itself and rested on her head. In another instant it was drawn slowly away, and, with a startled look, the half-weeping daughter rose and glided again to my side.

As I closed the door I thought of those words: "And the sins of the father shall be visited upon the children to the third and fourth generation."

CHAPTER XXIV

THE MARQUIS

But the events of the night are not over. As soon as I had seen mademoiselle comfortably ensconced in my old room up stairs, I returned to the sitting room, where the marquis still lingered. He was standing in the window when I entered, and turned with quite a bright face to greet me. But that brightness soon vanished as he met my glance, and it was with something like dismay that he commented upon my paleness, and asked if I were ill.

I told him I was ill at ease; that events of a most serious nature were transpiring in the house; that he was concerned in them heavily, grievously; that I could not rest till I had taken him into my confidence, and shown him upon what a precipice he was standing.

He evidently considered me demented, but as he looked at me longer, and noted my steady and unflinching gaze, he gradually turned pale, and uttered, in irrepressible anxiety, the one word—"Honora!"

"Miss Urquhart is well," I began, "and is as ignorant as yourself of the shadows that hover over her. She is all innocence and truth, sir. Honor, candor and purity dwell in her heart, and happiness in her eyes. Yet is that happiness threatened by the worst calamity that can befall a sensitive human being, and if you hold her in esteem—"

"Ma foi!" he broke in, with violent impetuosity. "I do not esteem her; I love her. What are these dreadful secrets? How is her happiness threatened? Tell me without hesitation, for I have entreated her to be my wife, and she—"

"She thinks it is a parent's whim, alone, which keeps her from responding fully to your wishes," I finished. "But madame's objections have deeper ground than that. Miserable woman as she is, she has some idea of honor left. She knew her daughter could not safely marry into a high and noble family, and so—"

"What is this you say?" came again in the quick and hurried tones of despair. "Mrs. Urquhart—"

"Wait," I broke in. "You call her Mrs. Urquhart, but she has no claim to that title. She and Edwin Urquhart have never been married."

He recoiled sharply, with a gesture of complete disbelief.

"How do you know?" he demanded. "They are strangers to you. I have known them in their own home. All the world credits their marriage, and—"

"All the world does not know what transpired in this house sixteen years ago, when Edwin Urquhart stopped here with his bride on his way to France."

He stared, seemed shaken, but presently hastened to remark:

"Ah, madame, you acknowledge that she is his wife. You said bride. One does not call a woman by that name without acknowledging a marriage service."

"The woman he brought here was his bride. Edwin Urquhart is no common criminal, Marquis de la Roche-Guyon."

It was hard to make him understand. It was hard to undermine his trust, step by step, inch by inch, till he found no hope, no shred of doubt to cling to. But it had to be done. If only to avert worse calamities and more heart-rending scenes, he must know at once, and before he took another step in relation to Miss Urquhart, just what her position was, and to what shame and suffering he was subjecting himself by accepting her love and pledging his own.

The task was not done till I had shown him this diary of mine, and related all that had just occurred in the room below. Then, indeed, he seemed to comprehend his position, and completely crushed and horror-stricken, subsided into a dreadful silence before me, the lines of years coming into his face as I watched him, till he became scarcely recognizable for the lordly and light-hearted cavalier whose dreams of love I had so fearfully interrupted some half hour or so before. From this lethargy of despair I did not seek to rouse him. I knew when he had anything to say he would speak, and till he had faced the situation and had made up his mind to his duty, I could wait his decision with perfect confidence in his fine nature and nice sense of honor.

You may, therefore, imagine my feelings when, after a long delay—an hour at least—he suddenly remarked:

"We have been a proud family. From time immemorial we have held ourselves aloof from whatever could be thought to stain our honor or impeach our good name. I cannot drag the unfathomable disgrace of all these crimes into a record so pure as that of the Roche-Guyon race. Though I had wished to bestow upon my wife a name and position of which she could be proud, I must content myself with merely giving her the comfort of a true heart and such support as can be provided by a loving but unaccustomed hand."

"Marquis—" I commenced.

But he cut my words short with a firm and determined gesture.

"My name is Louis de Fontaine," he explained. "Henceforth my cousin will be known as the marquis. It is the least I can do for the old French honor."

'Twas so simply, so determinedly done that I stood aghast as much at the serenity of his manner as the act which required such depth of sacrifice from one of his traditions and rearing.

"Then you continue to consider yourself the suitor of Miss Urquhart," I stammered. "You will marry her, though her parents may be called upon to perish upon the scaffold in an ignominy as great as ever befell two guilty mortals?"

The answer came brokenly, but with unwavering strength:

"Did you not say that she was innocent? Is she to be crushed beneath the guilt of her parents? Am I to take the last prop from one so soon to be bereft of all the supports upon which she has leaned from infancy? If I cling to her, she may live through her horror and shame; but should I fail her—great heavens! would we not have another life to answer for before God? Besides," he added, with the simplicity which marked his whole bearing, "I love her. I could not do otherwise if I would."

To this final word I could make no rejoinder. With a reverence unmingled with the taint of compassion, I took my departure, and being anxious by this time to know how my young charge was bearing her seclusion, I went to the room where I had left her, and softly opened the door.

CHAPTER XXV

MARK FELT

Subjected as I have been in the last three hours to distress and turmoil, I was delighted to find mademoiselle asleep, and to behold her peaceful face. Gazing at it, and noting the happy smile which unconsciously lingered on her lips, I could not but feel that, despite the hideous revelations which lay before her, her lot was an enviable one, allied as it promised to be with that of one of such high principles as the marquis. Though I am old now and have had my day, the love of the innocent and pure is sacred to me, and in this case it certainly has the charm of a spotless lily blooming in the jaws of hell.

As it was late and I was almost exhausted, I began to think of rest. But my uneasiness in regard to madame would not let me sleep till I had made another visit to her room. So, leaving the gentle sleeper lapped in serenest dreams, I proceeded to descend once more. As I passed the great clock on the stairs, I noticed that it was almost midnight and began to hasten my steps, when I heard a loud knock at the front door.

This is not an infrequent sound with us, but it greatly startled me this night. I even remember pausing and looking helplessly up and down the hall, as if it were a question whether I should obey the unwelcome summons. But such knocking as speedily followed could not be long ignored. So, subduing my impatience, I hastened to the door, and unlocking it, threw it open. A gust of rain and wind greeted me.

This was my first surprise, for I had not even noticed that the weather was unpleasant, so completely had I been absorbed by what had been going on in the house. My next was the bearing and appearance of the stranger who demanded my hospitality. For though both face and form were unknown to me, there was that in his aspect which stirred recollections not out of keeping with the unhappy subject then occupying all my thoughts. Yet I could not speak his name, or put into words the anticipations that vaguely agitated me, and led him through the hall and into the comfortable sitting room so lately vacated by the marquis, with no more distinct impression in my mind than that something was about to happen which would complete rather than interrupt the horrors of this eventful night.

And when the light fell full upon him, and I could see his eager eyes, this feeling increased, and no sooner had his cloak fallen from his shoulders and his hat left his head, than I recognized the prominent jaw and earnest face, and putting no curb on my impetuosity, I exclaimed at once, and without a doubt:

"Mr. Felt!"

The utterance of this name seemed to cause no surprise to my new guest.

"The same," he replied; "and you are Mrs. Truax, of course. Mr. Tamworth has described you to me, also this inn, till I feel as if I knew its every stone. I did not wish to visit it, but I could not help myself. An unknown influence has been drawing me here for days, and though I resisted it with all my strength, it finally became so powerful that I rose from my bed at night, saddled my horse, and started in this direction. I have been twenty hours on the road, but part of these I have spent in the thicket just over against you on the opposite side of the road. For the sight of the house awakened in my mind such a disturbance that I feared to show myself at the door. A voice out of the air seemed to cry, 'Not yet! not yet!' Nevertheless I could not go back nor leave the spot, which, once seen, possessed for me a fatal fascination."

I was speechless. Good God! were the old psychological influences at work, and had they acted upon him at forty miles distance?

"You come from Albany?" I at last stammered forth. "You must have had a wet time of it; it storms heavily, I see."

"Storms?" he repeated, glancing at the cloak he had thrown off. "Great Heaven! my cloak is saturated, and I did not even know it rained. A touch of the old spell," he murmured. "Something is about to happen to me; something has drawn me with purpose to this house."

I felt awe-struck. Would he guess next what that something was?

"At eleven o'clock," he went on, with the abstracted air of one recalling an experience, "I felt a pang shoot through my breast. I had been looking steadfastly at these walls, and somewhere about the building a light seemed to go out, for a pall of darkness suddenly settled upon it, simultaneously with the cessation of that imaginary cry which had hitherto detained me. Where was that light, Mrs. Truax, and what has happened here that I should feel myself called upon to cross this threshold to-night?"

I did not answer at once, for I was trembling. Was I to be subjected to another such an ordeal as I had experienced earlier in the evening and be forced to prepare, by such means as lay in my power, a much abused man for a most dreadful revelation? It began to look so.

"What has called me here?" he repeated. "Danger to her or death to him? They are thousands of miles away, and Tamworth could not have yet reached them, but peril of some deadly nature menaces them, I know. A stroke has gone home to him or her, and it is in this place I am to learn it; is it not so, Mrs. Truax?"

"Perhaps," I tremblingly assented. "There is a gentleman here from France who may be able to tell you something of the man and the woman you mean. Would it affect you very much to hear disastrous news of them?"

"I cannot say," he answered; "it should not. Mr. Tamworth tells me that he has acquainted you with the story of my life. Do you think I should feel overwhelmed at any retribution following a crime that was committed almost as much against me as against the pure and noble being who was the visible sufferer?"

"I shrink from answering," I returned; "the human heart is a curious thing. If he alone were to suffer—"

"Ah, he!" was the bitter ejaculation.

"Or if she," I proceeded, "were bound by no ties appealing to the sympathies! But she is a mother—"

"Good God!"

I had not thought it would affect him so, and stood appalled.

"A mother!" he repeated; "she! she! the tigress, the heartless one, with no more soul than the naked dagger I should have plunged into her breast and did not! Great Heaven! and this child has lived, I suppose; is grown up and—and—"

"Is the sweetest, purest, most unworldly of beautiful women that these eyes have ever rested upon."

I thought he would spring upon me, he leaned forward with so much impetuosity.

"How do you know?" he asked, and my heart stood still at the question.

"Because I have seen her," I presently rejoined. "Because I have had opportunities for studying her heart. She is called Honora, and she is like Miss Dudleigh, only more beautiful and with more claims to what is called character."

He did not seem to take in my words.

"You have been to France?" he declared.

"No," I corrected; "Miss Urquhart has been here."

He fell back, then started forward again, opened his lips and stared wildly, half fearfully about the room.

"Here?" he repeated, evidently overcome at the idea. "Why did they send her here? I should as soon have expected them to send her into the murk of the bottomless pit. A girl, an innocent girl, you say, and sent here?"

"They had reason; besides, she did not come alone."

This time he understood me.

"Oh!" he shrieked, "she in the house. I might have known it," he went on more calmly; "I did, only I would not believe it. Her crime has drawn her to the place of its perpetration. She could not resist the magnetic influence which all places of blood have upon the guilty. She has come back! And he?"

I shook my head.

"The man had less courage," I declared. "Perhaps because he was more guilty; perhaps because he had less love."

"Love?"

"It was love for the daughter which drew the mother here, not the spell of her crime or the accusing spirit of the dead. The woman who wronged you has some heart; she was willing to risk detection, and with it her reputation and life, to see if by any possibility she could venture to give happiness to the one being whom she really loves."

"Explain; I do not understand. How could she hope to find happiness for her child here?"

"By settling the question which evidently tortured her. By determining once for all whether the crime of sixteen years back had ever been discovered, and if she found it had not, to satisfy at once her own pride and her daughter's heart by giving that daughter to as noble a gentleman as ever carried a sword."

"And they are here now?"

"They are here."

"And she has discovered—"

"The futility of all her hopes."

He drew back, and his heavy breath echoed in deep pants through the room.

"What an end for Marah Leighton!" he gasped.

"What an end! And she is here!" he went on, after a moment of silent emotion—"under this roof! No wonder I felt myself called hither. And she knows her crime is detected? How came she to know this? Did you recognize her and tell her?"

"I recognized her and told her. There was no other course. We met in the secret chamber, whither she had come to make her own terrible investigations; and the sight of her there, on the spot where she had left the innocent to die, was too much for my sense of justice. I accused her to her face, and she crouched before me as under the lash. There was no possibility of denial after that, and she now lies—"

"Wait!" he cried, catching me painfully by the arm. "When was this day? To-day—to-night?"

"Not two hours ago."

His brow took on a look of awe.

"You see," he murmured, "she has power over me yet. When her hope broke, something snapped within me here. I abhor her, but I feel her grief. She was once all the world to me."

I recognized his right to emotion, and did not profane it by any words of mine. Instead of that I sought to leave him, but he would not let me go till he had asked me another question.

"And the daughter?" he urged. "Does she know of the opprobrium which must fall upon her head?"

"She sleeps," I replied, "with a smile of the shyest delight upon her lips. Her lover has followed her to this place, and the last words she heard to-night were those of his devotion. Her suffering must come to-morrow; yet it will be mitigated, for he will not forsake her, whatever shame may follow his loyalty. I have his word for that."

"Then the earth holds two lovers," was Mark Felt's rejoinder. "I thought it held but one." And with a sigh he let go my arm and turned to the window, with its background of driving rain and pitiless flashes of lightning.

I took the opportunity to excuse myself for a few minutes, and hurrying again into the hall, hastened, with nervous fear and an agitation greatly heightened by the unexpected interview I had just been through, to the now oft-opened door leading into the oak parlor.

I found it closed but not locked, and pushing it open, listened for a moment, then took a glance within. All was quiet and ghostly. A single candle guttering on the table at one end of the room lent a partial light by which I could discern the funereal bed and the other heavy and desolate-looking articles of furniture with which the room was encumbered. Honora's flowers, withering on the window seat, spoke of tender hopes not yet vanished from her tender dreams, but elsewhere all was hard, all was dreary, all was inexorably forbidding and cold. I shuddered as I looked, and shuddered still more as I approached the bed and paused firmly before it.

"Madame Letellier"—it was the only name by which I could bring myself to address her at that instant— "there is one gleam of brightness in your sky. The marquis knows the story of your guilt, yet consents to marry your daughter."

I received no reply.

Shaken by fresh doubts, and moved by an inexplicable terror, I stood still for a moment gathering up my strength, then I repeated my words, this time with sharp emphasis and scarcely concealed importunity.

"Madame," said I, "the marquis knows your guilt, yet consents to marry your daughter."

But the silence within remained unbroken, and not a movement displaced the somber falling curtains.

Agitated beyond endurance, I stretched forth my hands and drew those curtains aside. An unexpected sight met my eyes. There was no madame there; the bed was empty.

CHAPTER XXVI

FOR THE LAST TIME

My eyes turned immediately in the direction of the secret chamber. Its entrance was closed, but I knew she was hidden there as well as if the door had been open and I had seen her.

What should I do? For a moment I hesitated, then I rushed from the room and hastened back to Mr. Felt. I found him standing with his face to the door, eagerly awaiting my return.

"What has happened?" he asked, importunately. "Your face is as pale as death."

"Because death is in the house. Madame—"

"Ah!"

"Lies not in her bed, nor is she to be found in her room. There is another place, however, in which instinct tells me we shall find her, and if we do, we shall find her dead!"

"In her daughter's room? At her daughter's bedside?"

"No; in the secret chamber."

He gazed at me with wild and haggard aspect.

"You are right," he hoarsely assented. "Let us go; let us seek her; it may not be too late."

The entrance to this hidden room was closed, as I have said, and as I had never assisted at its opening, I did not know where to find the hidden spring by means of which the panel was moved. We had, therefore, to endure minutes of suspense while Mr. Felt fumbled at the wainscoting. The candle I held shook with my agitation, and though I had heard nothing of the storm before, it seemed now as if every gust which came swooping down upon the house tore its way through my shrinking consciousness with a force and menace that scattered the last remnant of self-possession. Not an instant in the whole terrible day had been more frightful to me, no, not the moment when I first heard the sliding of this very panel and the sound of her crawling form approaching me through the darkness. The vivid flashes of lightning that shot every now and then through the cracks of the closely shuttered window, making a skeleton of its framework, added not a little to its terror, there being no other light in the room save that and the flickering, almost dying flame, with which I strove to aid Mr. Felt's endeavors and only succeeded in lighting up his anxious and heavily bedewed forehead.

"Oh, oh!" was my moan; "this is terrible! Let us quit it or go around to my own room, where there is an open door."

But he did not hear me. His efforts had become frantic, and he tore at the wainscoting as if he would force it open by main strength.

"You cannot reach her that way," I declared. "Perhaps my hand may be more skillful. Let me try."

But he only increased his efforts. "I am coming, Marah; I am coming!" he called, and at once, as if guided by some angel's touch, his fingers slipped upon the spring. Immediately it yielded, and the opening so eagerly sought for was made.

"Go in," he gasped, "go in."

And so it was that the fate which had forced me against my will, and in despite of such intense shrinking, to pass so frequently into that hideous spot, where death held its revel and Nemesis awaited her victim, drove me thither once again, and, as I now hope, for the last time. For, there upon the floor, and almost in the same spot where we had found lying the remains of innocent Honora Urquhart, we saw, as my premonition had told me we should, the outstretched form of the unhappy being who had usurped her place in life, and now, in retribution of that act, had laid her head down upon the same couch in death. She was pulseless and quite cold. Upon her mouth her left hand lay pressed, as if, with her last breath, she sought to absorb the pure kiss which had been left there by the daughter she so much loved.

CHAPTER XXVII

A LAST WORD

Did Marah Leighton will the coming of her old lover to my inn on that fatal night? That is the question I asked, when, with the first breaking of the morning light, I discovered lying on the table under an empty phial, a letter addressed, not to her husband, nor to her child, but to him, Mark Felt. It is a question that will never be answered, but I know that he comforts himself with the supposition, and allows the trembling hope to pass, at times, across his troubled spirit, that in the bitterness of those last hours some touch of the divine mercy may have moved her soul and made her fitter for his memory to dwell upon.

The letter I afterward read. It was as follows:

TO THE MAN WHO GAVE ALL, BORE ALL, AND REAPED NOTHING BUT SUFFERING:

I am not worthy to write you, even with the prospect of death before me. But an influence I do not care to combat drives me to make you, of all men, the confidant of my remorse.

I did not perish sixteen years ago in the Hudson River. I lived to share in and profit by a crime that has left an indelible stain upon my life and an ineffaceable darkness within my soul. You know, or soon will know, what that crime was and how we prospered in it. Daring as it was dreadful, I heard its fearful details planned by his lips, without a shudder, because I was mad in those days, mad for wealth, mad for power, mad for adventure. The only madness I did not feel was love. This I say to comfort a pride that must have been sorely wounded in those days, as sorely wounded as your heart.

Edwin Urquhart could make my eyes shine and my blood run swiftly, but not so swiftly as to make me break my troth with you, had he not sworn to me that through him I should gain what moved me more than any man's love. How he was to accomplish this I could not see in the beginning, and was so little credulous of his being able to keep his oaths that I let myself be drawn by you almost to the church door.

But I got no further. There in the crowd he stood with a command in his eyes which forbade any further advance. Though I comprehended nothing then, I obeyed his look and went back, for my heart was not in any marriage, and it was in the hopes to which his looks seemed to point. Later he told me what those hopes were. He had been down to Long Island, and, while there, had chanced to hear in some tavern of the Happy-Go-Lucky Inn and its secret chamber, and he saw, or thought he saw, how he could make me his without losing the benefit of an alliance with Miss Dudleigh. And I thought I saw also, and entered into his plans, though they comprised crime and entailed horrors upon me from which woman naturally shrinks. I was hard as the nether millstone of which the Bible speaks, and went determinedly on in the path of dissimulation and crime which had been marked out for me, till we came to this inn. Then, owing, perhaps, to my long imprisonment in the dreadful box, I began to feel qualms of physical fear and such harrowing mental forebodings that more than once during that terrible evening I came near shouting for release.

But I was held back by apprehensions as great as any from which a premature release from my place of hiding could have freed me. I dared not face Honora, and I dared not subject Edwin Urquhart to the consequences of a public recognition of our perfidy, and so I let my opportunity go by, and became the sharer, as I was already the instigator, of the unheard-of crime by which I became, in the eyes of the world, his wife.

What I suffered during its perpetration no word of mine can convey. I cringed to her moans; I shook under the blow that stifled them. And when all was over, and the bolts which confined me were shot back, and I found myself once more on my feet and in the free air of this most horrible of rooms, I looked about, not for him, but her, and when I did not see her or any token of her death, I was seized by such an agony of revulsion that I uttered a great and irrepressible cry which filled the house, and brought more than one startled inquirer to our door.

For retribution and remorse were already busy within me, and in the lurking shadows about the fireplace I thought I saw the long and narrow slit made by the half-closed panel standing open between me and the secret place of her entombment. And though it was but an optical delusion, the panel being really closed, it might as well have been the truth, for I have never been able to rid myself of the sight of that chimerical strip of darkness, with its suggestions of guilt and death. It haunted my vision; it ruined my life; it destroyed my peace. If I shut my eyes at night, it opened before me. If I arrayed myself in jewels and rich raiment, and paused to take but a passing look at myself in the glass, this horror immediately came between me and my own image, blotting the vision of wealth from my eyes; so that I went into the homes of the noble or the courts of the king a clouded, miserable thing, seeing nothing but that black and narrow slit closing upon youth and beauty and innocence forever and forever and forever.

My child came. Ah! that I should have to mention her here! I do it in penance; I do it in despair; since with her my heart woke, and for her that heart is now broken, never to be healed again. Oh, if the knowledge of my misery wakens in you one thought that is not of revenge, cast a pitying eye upon this darling one, left in a hateful country without friends, without lover, without means. For friends and lover and means will all leave her with the revelations which the morning will bring, and unless Heaven is merciful to her innocence as it has been just to my guilt, she will have no other goal before her than that which has opened its refuge to me.

As for her father, let Heaven deal with him. He gave me this darling child; so I may not curse him, even if I cannot bless.

MARAH.

OCTOBER 23, 1791.

I have seen one bright thing to-day, and that was the faint and almost unearthly gleam which shot for a moment from beneath Honora's falling lids as I told her what love was and how the marquis only awaited her permission to speak to assure her of his boundless affection and his undying purpose to be true to her even to the point of assuming her griefs and taking upon himself the protection of her innocence.

If it had not been for this, I should have felt that the world was too dark to remain in, and life too horrible to be endured.

NOVEMBER 30, 1791.

I thought that when Honora Urquhart left my house to be married to M. De Fontaine, in the church below the hill, peace would return to us once more.

But there is no peace. This morning another horrible tragedy defiled my doorstep.

I was sitting in the open porch waiting for the mail coach, for it seemed to me that it was about time I received some word from Mr. Tamworth. It was yet some minutes before the time when the rumble of the coach is usually heard, and I was brooding, as was natural, over the more than terrible occurrences of the last few weeks, when I heard the clatter of horses' hoofs, and looking up and down the road, saw a small party of men approaching from the south. As they came nearer, I noticed that one of the riders was white-haired and presumably aged, and was interesting myself in him, when he came near enough for me to distinguish his features, and I perceived it was no other than Mr. Tamworth.

Rising in perturbation, I glanced at the men behind and abreast of him, and saw that one of these rode with lowered head and oppressed mien, and was just about to give that person a name in my mind when the horse he bestrode suddenly reared, bolted, and dashed forward to where I sat, flinging his rider at the very threshold of my house, where he lay senseless as the stone upon which his head had fallen.

For an instant both his companions and myself paused aghast at a sight so terrible and bewildering; then, amid cries from the road and one wild shriek from within, I rushed forward, and turning over the head, looked upon the face of the fallen man. It was not a new one to me. Though changed and seamed and white now in death, I recognized it at once. It was that of Edwin Urquhart.

This noon I took down the sign which has swung for twenty years over my front door. "Happy-Go-Lucky" is scarcely the name for an inn accursed by so many horrors.

FEBRUARY 3, 1792.

This week I have fulfilled the threat of years ago. I have had the oak parlor and its hideous adjunct torn from my house.

Now, perhaps, I can sleep.

MARCH 16.

News from Honora. The distant relative who succeeded to the estates and the title of the Marquis de la Roche-Guyon has fallen a victim to the guillotine. Would this have been the fate of Honora's husband had he forsaken her and returned home? There is reason to believe it. At all events, she finds herself greatly comforted by this news for the sacrifice which her husband made to his love, and no longer regrets the exile to which he has been forced to submit for her sake. Wonderful, wonderful Providence! I view its workings with renewed awe every day.

SEPTEMBER 5, 1795.

I have been from home. I have been on a visit to New York. I have tasted of change, of brightness, of free and cheerful living, and I can settle down now in this old and fast-decaying inn with something else to think about than ruin and fearful retribution.

I have been visiting Madame De Fontaine. She wished me to come, I think, that I might see how amply her married life had fulfilled the promise of her courtship days. Though she and her noble husband live in peaceful retirement, and without many of the appurtenances of wealth, they find such resources of delight in each other's companionship that it would be hard for the most exacting witness of their mutual felicity to wish them any different fate, or to desire for them any wider field of social influence.

The marquis—I shall always call him thus—has found a friend in General Washington, and though he is never seen at the President's receptions, or mingles his voice in the councils of his adopted country, there are evidences constantly appearing of the confidence reposed in him by this great man, which cannot but add to the exile's contentment and satisfaction.

Honora has developed into a grand beauty. The melancholy which her unhappy memories have necessarily infused into her countenance have given depth to her expression, which was always sweet, and frequently touching. She looks like a queen, but like a queen who has known not only grief, but love. There is nothing of despair in her glance, rather a lofty hope, and when her affections are touched, or her enthusiasm roused, she smiles with such a heavenly brightness in her countenance, that I think there is no fairer woman in the world, as I am assured there is none worthier.

Her husband agrees with me in this opinion, and is so happy that she said to me one day:

"I sometimes wonder how my heart succeeds in holding the joy which Heaven has seen fit to grant me. In it I read the forgiveness of God for the unutterable sins of my parents; and though the shadows will come, and do come, whenever I think upon the past, or see a face which, like yours, recalls memories as bitter as ever overwhelmed an innocent girl in her first youth, I find that with every year of love and peaceful living the darkness grows less, as if, somewhere in the boundless heavens, the mercy of God was making itself felt in the heart of her who once called herself my mother."

And hearing her speak thus, I felt my own breast lose something of the oppression which had hitherto weighed it down. And as the days passed, and I experienced more and more of the true peace that comes with perfect love and perfect trust, I found my tears turned to rejoicing and the story of my regrets into songs of hope.

And so I have come back comforted and at rest. If there are yet ghosts haunting the old inn, I do not see them, and though its walls are dismantled, its custom gone, and its renown a thing of the past, I can still sit on its grass-grown doorstep and roam through its fast-decaying corridors without discovering any blacker shadow following in my wake than that of my own figure, bent now with age, and only held upright by the firmness of the little cane with which I strive to give aid to my tottering and uncertain steps.

The grace of God has fallen at last upon the Happy-Go-Lucky Inn.

Anna Katharine Green – A Concise Bibliography

The Leavenworth Case (1878)
A Strange Disappearance (1880)
The Sword of Damocles: A Story of New York Life (1881)

The Defence of the Bride, and other Poems (1882)
X Y Z: A Detective Story (1883)
Hand and Ring (1883)
The Mill Mystery (1886)
7 to 12: A Detective Story (1887)
Risifi's Daughter, A Drama (1887)
Behind Closed Doors (1888)
Forsaken Inn (1890)
A Matter of Millions (1891)
The Old Stone House and Other Stories (1891)
Cynthia Wakeham's Money (1892)
Marked "Personal" (1893)
Miss Hurd: An Enigma (1894)
The Doctor, His Wife, and the Clock (1895)
Doctor Izard (1895)
That Affair Next Door (1897)
Lost Man's Lane: A Second Episode in the Life of Amelia Butterworth (1898)
Agatha Webb (1899)
The Circular Study (1900)
A Difficult Problem (1900)
One of my Sons (1901)
The Filigree Ball: Being a Full and True Account of the Solution of the Mystery Concerning the Jeffrey-Moore Affair (1903)
The Amethyst Box (1905)
The House in the Mist (1905)
The Millionaire Baby (1905)
The Chief Legatee' (1906)
The Woman in the Alcove (1906)
The Mayor's Wife (1907)
The House of the Whispering Pines (1910)
Three Thousand Dollars (1910)
Initials Only (1911)
Masterpieces of Mystery (1913)
Dark Hollow (1914)
The Golden Slipper, and Other Problems for Violet Strange (1915)
To the Minute; Scarlet and Black: Two Tales of Life's Perplexities (1916)
The Mystery of the Hasty Arrow (1917)
The Step on the Stair (1923)

www.ingramcontent.com/pod-product-compliance
Lightning Source LLC
Chambersburg PA
CBHW071406170626
46811CB00003B/1287